What Had Happened Was

Ah'Shay Young

WHAT HAD HAPPENED WAS

paperback ISBN: 9781955836241

eBook ISBN: 9781955836234

hardcover ISBN: 9781955836258

For my super-fan and big sister, Terasa N., who fell in love with my series and forced me continue writing to satisfy her friendship with the characters.

For my parents, my mother, Ruby, for making Momma J so easy to write and to my daddy, Douglas, for showing me what a Daddy's girl deserves. May they both rest in peace.

For daughters Dieeya, Mashyla, and Lamesha for putting up with me talking about the characters like they should know who they are.

And for my fiancé Laurenzo Y. for his support and making sure I had what I needed to write.

Acknowledgments

I would like to acknowledge my best friends Cassandra W. and Gina W. for being such an inspiration to the friend characters in this book. And my brother from another mother, Oda W., who inspired the character Otis.

Also my friend Tracey T., who was the first to read the book as I was writing it—including typos—and still say it's good and was always eager for more.

And my editor, publisher, and friend Lara B., without whom none of this would be possible. Not only did she make my dream come true, but she did it with pride and excitement the whole way through.

WHAT HAD HAPPENED WAS

Ah'Shay Young

www.admissionpress.com

I'm woke

It's crazy what we go through to keep love in our lives. We'll put up with things we tell others not to. We can give good advice but take none for ourselves. I'll never understand that. But hey, we're only human.

Chapter 1

How It Started

I think a lot of my issues with men stems from losing my dad at a young age. I was a toddler when he passed, so I don't remember his voice, his kisses, or his hugs. All I have are a few pictures of him posing with me and Momma, his hazel eyes shining with pride, his smile radiant and peaceful. He wasn't a huge man, but he was tall, my skin tone, and had muscular arms. She'd tell me stories about how he'd make up songs about her and tell her daily how beautiful she was. She says I'm a lot like him. I have his sense of humor, his eyes and smile. She'd boast about how he was so kind, smart, and never seemed to worry about anything. Whenever something would come up, he'd tell her, "You're with one of God's favorite children. Why you worried?" And things would always work out or fall into place.

Daddy didn't have any family. Like me, he was an only child and both his parents had passed before he ever met Momma. She said that's why we meant so much to him.

Whenever she speaks of him, her face is always filled with joy, but I can see the sadness behind her smile.

Momma had boyfriends as I grew up but no one she was ever serious about. She never got over the fact that Daddy passed a week before they were to get married, and she couldn't seem to get that attached to another man. She said she only had half a heart left and couldn't afford for it to be broken.

So, growing up I never saw my momma in love. I barely met any of the men she dated. And my mother's little sister, Auntie Renee, married for money. I vowed that wouldn't be me. I was going to have what my momma had with my daddy. I was going to fall in love.

Early on I guess I was looking for what I missed out on. I started out crushing on guys with light eyes. Didn't matter the color. The first was a boy named Johnathan. That lasted from first grade to fifth. My first kiss was with a boy named CJ Luis in eighth grade. He was light-skinned with light brown eyes. I don't know why I call it a kiss. It was really just a long peck on the lips.

When I started high school, things changed. It was all about the smile. I spent so many years of my life staring at my daddy's smile, I guess somehow it became a requirement.

I went from being the one crushing to being high school's most wanted. I developed everywhere. Most girls get the butt but not the breasts or vice versa. But I got both at the same time. With my daddy's eyes, long legs, caramel-colored skin, long, naturally curly hair, and full lips, every boy at school had their eyes on me. The only thing I didn't like was that I was so tall. Seemed like most of the cute guys were a couple inches under my 5'8". There were a few my height or taller.

One of them was David, the upper-class player. He was a little skinnier than I liked, and light-skinned with dark waves so deep they could make you seasick. That boy knew he was fine. He'd walk around with his designer clothes, brush in hand. He'd stop me in the hall and be brushing his waves the whole time as he put his mac down.

"What's up, baby? Why you always dissing me? You know I want you."

"Whatever, David. Talk to the hand," I'd say, blushing.

"We'd be hella fly together. You need to stop buggin'."

You read that right. That's how we talked in the 90s.

I liked him but not enough to be involved in all the shenanigans that came along with trying to be with him. He had way too many admirers. He chased me for years—even after he left high school. I figured it was because I was the only female who told him no.

The one I had the crush on was Malon. That boy there had me so gone. I remember the first time I saw him. He came dancing into the classroom right at the bell. He had a Jheri curl that was cut to have a long tail in the back with a little honey-blond dye on the ends, and he was swinging it from side to side. When the teacher called him out for being late, he smiled and that was the end of me. I learned his name when he got in trouble, and the teacher wrote his name on the board. He was super popular because of his talents. Not only could he rap and play basketball, but he could also dance too. That was another thing I guess I subconsciously wanted—an entertainer. My daddy claimed he was in a group called *Sultry Soul* and had a couple of hit records, though no one, including Momma, ever heard them. He told her all the records were lost over the years.

My first time even speaking to Malon was at one of our school dances. Now back then when we danced, we *danced*. We did stuff like the Running Man and the Humpty Dance. We were hot and sweaty as hell by the end of a song. And when we heard, "one and here comes the two to the three and four," everyone ran to the dance floor. The song was called "It's Funky Enough" by The DOC, and after people danced to that song, I had to agree. My best friend Kēssa and I were too busy following Malon and his friends around the room to get too sweaty. We had to keep it cute, but that song did make us move a little more than we had all night. Right after that, the DJ played "It's Something in my Heart" by Michel'le.

Malon and I made eye contact, but neither of us made a move toward each other.

"Girl, just go ask him to dance," Kēssa said, pushing me a little.

"No, I'm not about to ask no boy to dance with me."

"Look, Tina ain't got no shame in her game," Kēssa replied as we watched Tina ask him to dance. He shook his head no, and she walked off.

"Ooooh, he straight dissed her! Girl, gone over there before somebody else beats you to it!" she demanded, pushing me again.

I walked toward him, shaking like a leaf as he watched me. His friend whispered something to him, and I stopped, turned, and looked at Kēssa. She motioned for me to continue.

I stepped up to him and smiled. "Hey."

"What's up?" he asked with a nod and smile.

"Nothing."

"Yo' name Toi, right? You're in my history class."

"Yes."

"So, you wanna dance?"

"I mean, if you want to."

Hell, it was midway through the song, but I didn't care. He took my hand, walked me to the middle of the dance floor and pulled me close. I could smell his curl activator, and it smelled sweet. I looked around and saw other females staring at me with hate in their eyes. Especially Tina and her crew. But I didn't care. All that mattered was I was being held by the boy of my dreams, and he had his hands on my booty.

After that our relationship was weird. I liked him and he liked me, but he couldn't be with me because he was a senior and I was a sophomore. I think his friends was in his ear about it. Half of them had tried and failed, so they didn't want to see him get me. I found out that this girl named Shay who sat next to me in one of my classes was his little sister. We were cool and eventually became friends, which gave me an excuse to go over to his house. And I made sure to go over there every day. Now don't get me wrong—Shay and I were cool, but I was after him.

One day while Kēssa and I was over there with Shay, we were sitting in the living room going over some stuff from class and gossiping about boys when Malon come waltzing in with his shirt off showing his little muscles.

"Ugh, why you come in here lookin' like that?" Shay asked, turning up her nose.

"I'm not worried about you and yo' company. I got some moves to practice."

"Boy, we trying to study. Go do that in yo' room."

"Y'all wasn't studying. I heard Kēssa tellin' you about Carl liking you. Stop lying. Y'all go in yo' room," he said, poppin' a tape into the VCR.

"Y'all, let's go back here," Shay suggested.

"No, he's not going to run me up out of here," I stated. I wasn't going anywhere. I had to see whatever moves he was about to practice. I could feel my hormones raging and the excitement building.

"Me either," Kēssa agreed, eyes shining.

I rolled my eyes. Kēssa has been my best friend since childhood. We grew up down the street from each other. She's short, light-skinned, and kept the latest hairstyles. By high school she looked like the singer Mya. She didn't have much of a body, but her looks got her all the attention she needed. Just didn't seem to be from the guys she wanted. My only problem with her is that she copied me. A lot. She wanted to wear what I wore and talk like I talked. Sometimes I would be saying something and catch her moving her lips like she was a ventriloquist dummy or something. I didn't know if she was trying to compete with me or what. Like she wanted to see if she could get a guy before I did. It happened so often that we made a rule about it later. But I let her know straight up that Malon was mine. I didn't care what she was feelin'.

He turned on Johnny Gill's "Rub You the Right Way" video and started mimicking his moves. I wasn't sure why he chose to perform this particular song since I always thought Johnny Gill looked crazy in a majority of the moves he did in that video. Johnny is a singer not a dancer. But Malon put his own little spin on everything, and it was cute or whatever until the part where Johnny started singing about rubbing with his magic hands and showing what you're missin' in a man, and that boy started moving and thrusting in a way that almost made me fall off the couch. He was looking dead at me too. I didn't know it at the time but the feelin' he gave me was called lust.

Later that night, Malon came back out of his room.

"Hey, Toi, come here a second," he requested, interrupting our conversation.

I couldn't believe he was calling for me. I slowly walked up to him in the hall. He took my hand and escorted me to his room and closed the door. It was dark except from the lights dancing on his stereo as it played "Right and Wrong Way" by Keith Sweat.

I sat down on his bed, nervous as hell. I didn't know what was about to happen. Mind you, I was still a virgin at the time. First thing that came to mind was he was going to try and get some. Would I let him? We had never even had a conversation before. I mean, I'd had plenty of conversations with him by this time, he just wasn't privy to any of them.

He sat down next to me. "I see how you always lookin' at me."

"Ain't nobody lookin' at you."

"Yeah, you lookin'. I thought you were hookin' up with Rovere. He always up in yo' face."

"Boy, please. Rovere isn't even my type. He's just the homeboy."

"That's what's up. You fine though. I haven't forgotten about our little moment at the dance. I was waiting for you to come over there instead of watching me from a distance." He put his hand on my thigh.

"Why didn't you come up to me?" I said, blushing and screaming "OH MY GOD" in my head.

"I wanted to see how much you liked me. But you haven't said nothing since."

"You haven't either."

"I walk by yo' locker every day. My locker way on the senior side. Who you think I'm over there for?"

"I don't know."

"I was trying to get yo' attention."

"You been had that. You're the man, you're supposed to approach me."

"Well, I'm approaching you now. So, what's up?" he asked, getting closer. I felt a pulsing in my clit. That had never happened before.

Right then Shay knocked on the door and said that my momma was outside. We didn't have cell phones at the time so Momma would drop us off and pop up whenever she felt like it to pick us up. Bad timing for me, but good Momma timing because something was about to go down.

"Dang, I wanted to get to know you. I guess I'll see you tomorrow then," Malon said.

"Yelp," I said, nodding, not sure what else to say as I looked down at the floor. But I hadn't got up yet. I was frozen in place. Finally, he turned my head up toward his and kissed me. Not a quick peck. Like he tongued a sista down. That was actually my first real kiss. It was good, too, I'm not gone lie. But the next thing I knew he was laying me back on the bed and getting on top of me. I laid there with my legs pressed together kissing him back as he basically dry humped me.

"Toi! Yo' momma said bring your tail on!" Shay yelled through the door. I was upset and relieved at the same time.

He eased off me, and I hurried to my feet. "Bye."

And that was it. I couldn't wait to get home to tell Kēssa all about it.

Malon and I started talking on the phone, and we'd go in his room whenever his momma wasn't there and make out. He'd feel me up, I'd feel him up, but it never went any further than that. For whatever reason, as soon as we'd get to school, it would be like he didn't know me at all.

Kēssa thought it was wrong for him to act like we weren't

kickin' it every day, and that he didn't deserve my time. She kept saying I should hook up with Samir and leave Malon alone.

When she told me about Samir, I didn't know who she was talking about. All I could see was Malon, so I never paid any attention to anyone else. You know that's how it always goes: I-want-you-but-you-want-him type of stuff. Anyways, Samir was in our French class, so she pointed him out. He was cute. A couple of inches taller than me, dark smooth skin, straight babyface, and hair cut extra low. Even at that time, you could tell he worked out. But once again it was his smile that attracted me. His teeth were white as pearls, and his lips were full and perfectly proportioned.

One day right after French class, Kēssa said, "Girl, Samir asked about you all through class. He wouldn't leave me alone. He was all like, 'Did you tell her about me asking about her? Do you think she likes me? Did she say I was cute? Ask her if I can get her phone number.' He gave me this note to give to you." She handed me a folded piece of paper.

"I mean, it's all good. But I don't know him. He never says anything to me."

"He's hella cool, he's funny. I think y'all would be a cute couple."

Later I read the note and it said:

> I know you don't know me, but I think you are all that and a bag of chips. I stare at you every day telling myself that you're finally gone notice me but all I get is a smile. I would approach you but by the time I try some dude always up in yo' face, so I just bounce. Here's my number at the crib. Call me sometimes.

I thought it was cute, so I called him a few days later and we hit it off right away. He was sweet and funny.

Samir was the one that I stayed up with all night on the phone. Momma would sometimes pick up the phone and embarrass me.

"I know you don't have your fast ass on my phone this time of the night! If you don't get your ass off this phone . . . !" she'd yell through her teeth.

He would do things like play songs for me. Our favorite ones were, "Smile," "Let's Chill," and "Tease Me Tonight" by Guy. He even gave me the pet name "Smile" because we loved that song so much. I can't listen to those songs anymore to this day.

My mom liked him a lot. He was such a charmer and always respectful, with "yes, ma'am" and "no, ma'am." She used to tell me how sweet she thought he was. She didn't even trip about him being my boyfriend once she got to know him. After a while he was at my house on the daily. Momma got so used to him being there she made dinner for all three of us most nights. On the weekends they'd sometimes play spades together, laugh, and talk shit. Felt like he was a part of our family.

The other thing I liked about Samir is that he had a car. It was cool to be seen leaving with my man after school. I would hook up my friends with his friends, and we'd get in his car and go here and there. Music loud. Whenever we'd stop at a red light, he wouldn't move unless I kissed him. I mean he literally would sit at the green light with people honking their horns until I kissed him. I thought that was cute. Didn't know it was a sign of crazy.

The first year was magical. My first time having sex wasn't though. His mom had gone out of town. I told my mom that I was going to spend the night at Kēssa's. We hadn't talked about it, but I pretty much knew it was going to happen. He picked me up from Kēssa's, and we went over to his house. He had cooked me a spaghetti dinner, lit candles and all. I couldn't eat though because I was too nervous. The old-school song "Tonight Is the Night" by Betty Wright kept playing over and over in my head. Would tonight be the night he made me a woman?

Anyways, after dinner we sat on the couch, and he started

playing music. We slow danced and he kept grinding on me which kinda annoyed me, but I wasn't sure why. I could feel his hardness though. I don't know if I've ever been that nervous before, other than that night with Malon. Somehow, he slow danced me into his bedroom. We fell back on his bed kissing and before I knew it, he had raised my little pink mini skirt, pushed my panties to the side, and worked his way inside me. I didn't know how to feel or what to do so I just let him do whatever. It did hurt some. He pumped and pumped, then suddenly pulled out real fast and it was over. I was happy when it ended. It wasn't like I thought it would be. And honestly it didn't feel that good. I couldn't understand why everyone made such a big deal about having sex.

Afterward, we laid together and talked about what if . . . what if I got pregnant and how good of a dad he would be. All I know is I was scared to death that would happen. We talked until we both fell asleep.

We didn't talk about or have sex again until we were well into our second year together. And I thought we were all good. But after the second time we had sex, I started to notice things about him I didn't like. For one, he had a jealous streak. We went to John Marshall High School (Bears for life!) and we all had IDs with our pictures on them. At the end of the year, guys would give their IDs to the girl that they liked. Malon gave me his ID before he graduated. When Samir saw that I had it, he took a hole puncher to it. Punched the boy's face right out. I was mad. I found the little piece and put it back in the best I could. We fought about that for a week. Then he stole my journal, went and found one of the guys I wrote about—mind you this was well before Samir was in my life —and tried to fight him. That confused the hell out of me.

Another issue I had with Samir was that he was always at my house, but I didn't get to spend much time at his unless his mom and sister were gone. I only met them twice. They would sometimes answer the phone when I called but we weren't on speaking terms. I knew his cousin BK better than either of them. I wasn't able to build a relationship with his mom the way he did with mine. I still don't know what he was hiding.

Toward the end of the relationship, things just got to be too much. Two major things happened that I won't ever forget.

The first incident happened at a party. Samir's cousin BK and my friend Nyah lived in some apartments in Midwest City, and they were having an apartment party. Everyone participated and some people even opened their doors for people to just come and go as they pleased. Still to this day I don't know how you can just open your door and let people in and out of your house. That takes a lot of trust. But everyone seemed to know each other well enough, I guess. They had snacks and drinks and you just helped yourself. I had never experienced a party like that. They made it sound so cool and exciting.

"Smile, I know you don't like parties, but you know people in the apartments. And I promise you there will be no shooting or fighting. We do this every year!" Samir told me.

"Really though, it is all that!" his cousin BK chimed in. "In the back is the old-school peeps who play games, listen to their old-school music, and watch the little kids because it's right by the park. In the front is where I'll be at with all the young hoes and the rap music."

"See, that's why you and Kim broke up. You always chasin' hoes," Kēssa said.

"Mind yo' bizness! You always got something to say, dang!" Samir said. Sometimes I didn't know if they were joking or not.

"Y'all hate the truth," she answered back, and we laughed.

"Naw, for real, it's all good! You gotta bome and bheck it out," BK said, changing every c to a b. Bloods don't say things with a c unless it's ck. It's a long story.

"Yeah, let's go, sis! I need to find me a baller," Kēssa said.

"Don't nobody want your bighead ass," BK said, laughing.

Between the three of them, they talked me into it. I later wished I wouldn't have gone.

~

THE DAY OF THE PARTY, NYAH PICKED US UP. SHE AND Kēssa were so hyped. "Girl, I know you don't like people, but these parties are always fun! I'm telling you, you're going to love this!" Nyah said to me, dancing in her seat. She and Kēssa were high-fiving and everything.

We got to Nyah's around seven p.m. In the summertime in Oklahoma, it doesn't even start getting dark till around eight thirty at night. People were already walking around, playing music, and eating.

"The party has begun, y'all!" Nyah said as we were getting out of the car. "I gotta get in here and finish getting dressed!" She ran to the door.

Kēssa and I turned on TLC's tape Oooooh . . . On the TLC Tip and had a little wine cooler to get us in a party mood. Samir and BK showed up.

"Y'all ready?" BK asked. He was dressed in all red from head to toe. That made me nervous because I knew he was claiming to be a Blood and at the time people were getting shot for claiming sets. I wanted to speak up but apparently it didn't bother no one but me, so I kept quiet.

"We just chillin' right now. Waiting on Nyah to get ready," I answered.

"Come here, baby," Samir said, pulling me into one of the kid's rooms. "Do you mind if I just hang with BK tonight, and you hang with your friends?"

"No, that's fine. I know that he plans on being with the hoes though," I replied with a little side-eye.

"You know I'm not worried about no hoes. You can come and find me any time and give me love."

"Whatever, I wasn't planning on being up under you anyway." We laughed and kissed and went back in the living room with everyone else.

Soon the party was in full swing, and people were everywhere.

Looking out the window, I could see people were smoking weed, drinking, going from one side of the apartments to the other, kids chasing each other and running down to the pool. Everyone was smiling and playing and dancing. It was a vibe. Nice to see a bunch of black people getting along and having a good time.

Just before it started getting dark, Nyah finally was ready to head out. We joined others, dancing and walking here and there. Things were all good. Not one fight had broken out. After dark, we made our way to the front of the apartments where guys were. We saw Samir's car and a bunch of females around it, but no Samir and no BK. Nyah noticed that Samir's car door was open on the opposite side of the car.

"Is Samir or BK in there?" Nyah asked, bending forward, squinting, trying to see.

"His light isn't on, so I can't see who's in there. It's probably BK with all those females over there," I answered.

We walked over to see who was in my man's car. My stomach was in knots. He did say I could pop up whenever, so I calmed myself with that thought. I mean, he wouldn't be that stupid, right?

I walked around to the driver's door, and I seen him in the car with some bitch straddling him in the driver's seat. The pain and anger hit me, and I felt as though I had blacked out for a second.

"Oh, so this what we doin'?" I yelled and stormed away. Before I got completely gone, I saw him throw her to the ground and hop out of the car to come after me. My ears were ringing, and I could hardly hear anyone.

Kēssa was asking me, "What's wrong? What happened?" over and over. I couldn't speak.

Samir kept saying, "Smile, come here! Smile! Toi, let me talk to you!"

But I kept walking till I was away from all the people and music. He finally caught up with me. BK, Nyah, and Kēssa were right behind him.

I sat down on something. I don't even know what. He ran up

to me, trying to explain. "I know what you thinking, baby, but it's not like that! I was just sitting there talking to her and she thought it was funny to hop in on top of me and as soon as she did it you just walked up!" He talked fast as hell. I said nothing.

"Really? That's what happened?" Kēssa asked, sounding doubtful.

"Man, why don't you gone somewhere!" Samir shouted at Kēssa.

"Come on, Kēssa, Nyah. Let's let them talk." BK tried to pull them away.

"I'm not going nowhere with him all up in her face like that!" Nyah answered, rolling her neck.

"Can you tell them we good so we can talk?" Samir yelled.

I looked at them, then gave Nyah a look like, *Don't go far*. I was so busy fighting back tears that all I could do was look at her.

"We gone be right over here if you need us, girl," Nyah said as they moved a few feet away.

"Are you going to look at me?" He still had a tone in his voice.

"I don't have to look at you to hear you." I gave the attitude right back. He was acting like *I* did something wrong.

"Man, I promise you that's what happened, but I guess you're still mad, huh?"

"You shouldn't have even been entertaining her in the first place. What the hell were you talking to her about that made her feel comfortable enough for her to play with you like that?"

"We weren't talking about nothing! I don't know why she felt she could do that! So, you still mad?" I knew he could see I was still mad.

"Nope. Gone back and have a good time," I answered, waving him away from me.

"Naw, because you still mad! You know how much I love you! I wouldn't disrespect you knowing you right around here and could show up at any time. I'm not stupid!"

"Oh, so not something you would do if I'm close by. Gotcha."

"See, now you're really buggin'! That's not what I meant!"

I sat there not looking at him, and he just stood there staring at me. After I don't know how long he said, "I'm not going to stand here while you're acting like this. If you that mad, we can just end it right here." That's when I did look at him and shrugged my shoulders. He turned to BK. "Man, come on. Let's go. She buggin'," and they walked away.

We didn't use words like narcissist back then, but I do realize now that's what I was working with. Hindsight is always 20/20.

Kēssa asked, "Are you okay, sis?"

"I'm good. I'm just ready to go," I said, voice trembling.

"No, we are not going to let him ruin our fun! Come on. BK said there is some Jell-O shots in this apartment over here. Let's go get us some," Nyah said, and they both pulled me to my feet. I went along with them, the whole time trying not to cry. How could he up and end it like that after he messed up? He should've been kissing my ass!

We found the apartment with the Jell-O shots. The lady that was in there greeted us and said, "Help yourselves," and we took about three shots each. They must have been strong because I remember feeling them right away. We walked outside the apartment door and there were couples slow dancing. I could see Samir's car from where I was but couldn't see him or the other female. The way he dropped her on the ground to come chase me, you'd think she'd leave him alone. But it's whatever since he ended it, right?

Standing with my eyes closed, feeling the breeze, the shots, and the music, I remember the song, "I Don't Wanna Do Anything Else" by Mary J and KC was on. I was still fighting back tears when this tall guy walked up to me. He said his name was Mark, but I don't remember what he looked like. I do remember he had on an army uniform. I didn't feel like speaking, so I didn't even give him my name. Mark asked me to dance with him, and I was like, *Why not?*

We slow danced and he tried to ask me questions, but I was

tipsy and in my feelings, so he wasn't getting much conversation out of me.

The next thing I knew Kēssa shouted, "Toi, here comes Samir!"

I didn't care, but I still looked over Mark's shoulder to see him coming. The look on Samir's face was the scariest thing I've ever seen. My pulse pounded in my ears. He was coming fast, furious, and I didn't know if he was coming for Mark or me. I stood watching', paralyzed.

Just before he got to us, he screamed, "This nigga got me fucked up, fam!" The anger on his face made him unrecognizable.

BK ran full-speed toward Samir and hollered, "No, fam! No! Wait! Somebody stop him!"

I continue dancing, panicking inside and praying he didn't make it to us.

"Wait nothing! I'm going to kill him!" Samir shouted.

Poor Mark had no idea what was coming his way. He whispered to me, "Sounds like someone is about to start fighting," and shook his head.

You about to start fighting or get yo' ass whooped.

The next thing I knew, BK tackled Samir and dragged him off. I was so relieved. I hurried and thanked Mark for the dance, and we three females went straight for Nyah's car. As we were getting in the car to leave, here comes Samir and BK.

"Wait! Where you think you going?" Samir shouted at me, and we hurried into the car. I wasn't sure what he was going to do, and I wasn't going to stand there and find out. We locked the doors. I looked in the side mirror and saw BK still trying to hold him back. "If you leave, I'm going to find that nigga and beat the shit out of him! Come talk to me NOW!"

"Samir, chill! Damn!" BK shouted.

"You can do whatever you want. I'm going home," I said from the safety of the car.

He calmed down enough for BK to let him go. He walked up to the car window, which was down just enough for him to say what he wanted to say but not enough for him to be able to reach in.

He took a deep breath and lowered his voice. "Look, baby, I'm not even mad. I just didn't like seeing his arms around you like that. Can I just follow you home?"

"No, not tonight. I'm done right now," I said as Nyah started the car.

"Baby, for real. We need to talk about this shit right now!" he said through his teeth, trying not to show his agitation.

"There is nothing to talk about. Nyah, can we go, please?"

As she put the car in drive, he punched the window and kicked the side of the car. That scared me so bad.

"Mutha fucka! You betta stop GEEKIN'!" Nyah screamed.

He then started yanking on the door handle. "Get yo' ass out this car! You not going nowhere!" he insisted. "I said we gone talk about this! You got me fucked up! Letting that nigga touch all on you in my face! OPEN THIS DAMN DOOR!"

BK grabbed him again and Nyah drove off. I looked back and Samir was pushing BK, trying to get him off of him, and screaming at us to come back.

SAMIR CAME BY THE HOUSE THE NEXT DAY. I TOLD Momma to tell him I wasn't home. He was blowing up Kēssa's phone till her momma cussed him out. He even tried to get Nyah to call me from her phone, but she refused.

She called me. "Girl, Samir just left here. He wanted me to call you and then just put him on the phone. He was crying and begging. I don't know what you did to him, but he really loves you."

"I don't call anything that happened last night love. I didn't recognize him the way he was acting. That was scary! He broke up with me after he messed up and then gets mad when he sees me slow dancing with someone else? On top of that, punching the car window the way he did. How I know he wouldn't of hit me? I'll pass on that kind of love. He can wait till I decide I want to talk to him. If I decide that."

"I feel you. I'm not saying you're wrong for not talking to him. He said he reacted like that because he was trying to get you to talk to him when he said to end it. You know he didn't mean that. He was drunk, but he wasn't going to hurt you. But he probably would have hurt that guy you were dancing with." I didn't respond so she continued, "I think you should talk to him. I told him to give you some time though."

I didn't care what she said. I loved him but that was uncalled for. I didn't talk to him for a couple of weeks. Then one day, he drove by the house when Momma and I were taking groceries in. He jumped out and helped. Honestly, I still wasn't ready to see or talk to him. The look on his face when he saw me dancing with Mark and when he was trying to open the car door messed me up.

We finished helping Momma put the bags in the house. I still hadn't looked at him or said two words to him. Momma called me into her room.

"Go talk to that boy. Got him walking around here looking like a sad little puppy."

I had told Momma what had happened but not the full story. If she knew about how far his anger got out of control, she wouldn't be telling me to talk to him. She probably would've shot him. My momma keeps a gun.

"I didn't tell him to come over here."

"Go talk to him," Momma said through her teeth.

I put my head down and slowly walked down the hall. I got to the living room, and he wasn't there so I looked outside. There he was sitting on the porch. I went out and sat on the opposite side.

"Why are you here?" I asked, staring at the ground.

"You won't answer my calls. It's been two weeks! I haven't seen or talked to you. I miss you!"

"I thought we broke up."

"You know I didn't mean that shit. I was just mad because

you were acting like you couldn't listen to me." He got up and squatted down in front of me. "You still won't even look at me. You hate me, huh?"

"You know I don't hate you. I was hurt more than once by you that night and then you acting all scary like you wanted to hit me or something."

"Smile, look at me." He took my hands in his. I looked up into his eyes. "I would never put my hands on you! I love you! I was scared I was going to lose you over some dumb shit. I swear, it happened that fast. I got into the car to change the tape and she jumped into my lap and before I could get her off me you walked up! I swear that's how it happened! I'm sorry, baby! I didn't have time to respond. I wasn't studdin' those hoes. I know what I got."

He reached into his pocket and pulled out a gold nugget ring and put it on my finger. "I don't want nobody but you." He pulled me to my feet and hugged me. "You know I love you! Please forgive me. I swear that was nothing."

My dumb ass fell for it too.

Chapter 2

How It Ended

I don't remember if it was three or four months later when I got heartbroken for the last time by Samir. Things were going just as good as before. I still had some trust issues with him, so I wouldn't give him none. But for about two to three weeks he would come over and chill with me but said he had to be home by a certain time because his mom had started working nights. She didn't want him not to be there at night, scared someone might break in. I understood that, and it kept him from begging me to do something I didn't want to do. I would call him, and we'd still talk most of the night away. Some nights he wouldn't answer and later say he just fell asleep early from boredom. I didn't trip, but it did feel like we were growing distant. When I would talk to him about it, he would just say that it was all in my mind.

Out of the blue one day, I got a call from his sister.

"Toi, this is Crissy. I need to talk to you about Samir. I hope you won't hate me after this, but you should know." She spoke quickly. I could hear in her voice something was wrong. Very wrong.

I took a seat as a crazy nervous feeling started churning in my stomach, and I immediately began to feel nauseous. My mind started swimming with all kinds of bad thoughts. Is he in jail or the hospital?

"What's up, Crissy?" I asked nervously.

She took a deep breath. "I don't know how to tell you this. This is going to hurt. I know you think he loves you, but he doesn't deserve you." Long pause. "Okay, I'm just going to say it. He got some girl pregnant and has moved her into Momma's house!" she finally blurted out. "Momma just found out and told me about it yesterday. You know Momma started working nights, so apparently she's been there every night and just leaving before Momma gets home. I'm sorry, Toi, but you deserve to know. I would want someone to tell me."

I was shaken to the core. "Does he know you told me?"

"No, and I would appreciate you not telling him I told you."

"I won't, I promise."

I sat holding the phone even after she was gone, the loud *ungg-ungg-ungg* of the disconnect tone in my ear. I believed every word she said without question because who would call someone they barely knew with that type of lie. I finally turned the phone off, then immediately back on. Hands shaking, I called Kēssa and Nyah on three-way to give them the 411.

"Fo' real tho! He hasn't said anything to you?" Kēssa asked.

"No," I said, voice catching in my throat.

"How she get your number?" she asked.

"I'm sure it was on the Caller ID. I don't know."

"Did she say how far along this girl is?" Nyah asked.

"No. She just said I deserve to know," I replied.

"We going over there tonight since he don't know she told you. We'll see," Nyah said.

I called him at eight p.m., trying so hard not to let him hear the pain in my voice.

"What you doing?" I asked when he answered.

"Nothing. Chillin'. Not feeling good so . . ." he said, adding a fake cough and a sniffle.

"What's wrong, baby?" I asked, not concerned at all.

"Think I'm getting a cold or something. I don't know. I'm going to take some medicine and go to bed."

I knew he was lying. "You want me to come over and take care of you?"

"No!" he shouted and cleared his throat. "I mean, naw. You don't have to do all that. Besides, I don't want to get you sick."

He was for sure lying.

I knew his mom left for work around ten p.m. Nyah and Kēssa came and got me a little after nine fifteen. We got to his mom's and sat outside, waiting to see her leave.

"What am I supposed to tell him why I popped up?" I asked the girls, nervous about the whole situation.

"Tell him you came because he said he was sick, and you just wanted to be sure he's okay," Kēssa answered. "He's your man. Hell, you don't need a reason. He pops up at your house all the time so he shouldn't have a problem with you popping up, right?"

"Yeah, but I've never done it."

"So. You doing it now," Nyah said as we watched his mom get in her car and leave.

We sat outside a while to see if anyone came to the door, but no one ever did.

"Maybe he really is sick. Doesn't look like the girl is coming over," I said, feeling a little bit of relief not seeing anyone so far.

"The bitch could of climbed in the window. We don't know how she gettin' in."

"This just feels wrong," I said.

"Well, start feelin' right about it. We goin' in there. You need to do this for your own peace of mind," Nyah told me.

We waited another twenty minutes and went to the door. I knocked and heard him.

"Who is it?" he shouted.

"It's me!" I shouted back.

"Oh, umm, hold on!"

We could hear him mumbling, and we all gave each other a look that confirmed we heard the same thing.

Finally, the lock turned, and he popped the door open. "Baby, what are y'all doing here?" he asked, eyes darting.

"You said you were sick. I know you said you didn't need me to check on you, but I was concerned." I pushed past him and walked into the house with the girls right behind me.

"I took some medicine, like I said, and I'm feeling somewhat better."

He shut the door and walked over to hug me. I tried to relax and not stiffen up, since that would cause him to wonder what was wrong. I needed him to feel like I was good.

The girls took a seat on the couch, and I stood in the threshold to the hallway that led to his room.

"Are you going to sit down?" he asked. I ignored his question and stood there. He turned to go into the kitchen. "Y'all want something to drink?" He opened the refrigerator.

Kēssa and Nyah said ice water at the same time. Once he started moving around in the kitchen, I saw that as my chance to get ahead of him and go to his room to see if someone was hiding in there.

"I forgot. I left my jacket the last time we were here. I'm just going to go get it," I said, already walking down the hall to his room. I have no idea why I had to lie or announce it. Would've made more sense to just walk back there.

He slammed the refrigerator door and dropped a glass. "Fuck! Wait, baby! My room isn't clean!"

I heard him coming and picked up my step. "Boy, your room isn't ever clean. Stop buggin'."

By the time he got to me, I had already opened the door and turned on the light. There she was, laying on his bed, wearing boxers and a bra, hiding in the dark. She looked to be around six or seven months pregnant because her belly was huge. My heart was beating so fast I thought it might jump out of my chest. He'd been with this chick a long time apparently. Why did he even come to my house and beg me to get back with him? I stood there staring at her. I don't know if I even blinked.

"Baby, I can explain . . ." he said, looking at her too.

"Oh, so this the bitch you hiding me from?" she asked, standing up off the bed. "I don't know why I even stayed back here."

"Don't do that! You not gone disrespect my woman like that!" he had the nerve to say. Like he hadn't already shown me the ultimate disrespect.

"Your woman? She wasn't your woman last night! She wasn't your woman when you were trying to fuck me right befo' she got here! She's not carrying yo' baby, but I am!" she yelled back at him.

"Word?" I asked, looking at him.

"Bitch, shut up!" He got all up in her face as Nyah and Kēssa walked up and peered over my shoulder.

"That's a damn shame. Girl, you need to kick him to the curb," Nyah whispered, shaking her head, watching them argue in front of us.

"Let's go." I turned to leave.

We hurried toward the door, leaving them in the throes of their showdown.

My knees buckled a little, but it didn't mess up my stride. All I wanted to do was get away before I broke down. I've never been so humiliated and hurt in my life, and I didn't want the person who caused it to have the pleasure of seeing me cry.

"Baby, wait! PLEASE!"

I looked back and saw him speed-walking toward us. We all hopped into the car, closing the doors in sync and locking them. I was hoping we didn't have a repeat of last time since BK wasn't there to help us. I don't know why Nyah sat there with the car running, giving him time to catch up to us.

He ran up to Nyah's window first. "Nyah, don't drive off! Give me a sec, please!" He put his hands together and made his begging face.

"Okay, but if you so much as blink wrong, I'm driving off. You put a dent in my door last time," Nyah said, not moving.

He ran around to my side of the car. "Can you roll the window down please, baby?" I cracked the window. "Are you going to let me talk to you? I didn't want you to find out like this! It was a mistake, but when her mom found out she was pregnant she kicked her out!"

"How is anything you're saying to me right now supposed to mean something? She been pregnant for months! Not one time do I remember you telling me you cheated on me. Which makes me wonder how many times that happened."

"It was just that one time."

"And last night. It was happening or about to happen before I got here."

He hung his head.

"You right, I know. I fucked up. This is bad. I couldn't tell you because I didn't want to lose you."

Why do men think saying that is a good thing? A person can be so damn selfish that they do you dirty and still feel they deserve to keep the relationship. Make that make sense.

"So you lie to me and cheat on me instead? I'm so stupid I would never find out, huh?" Silence. "You no longer have to explain anything to me. You can save all that for your baby momma. Nyah, let's go."

As we drove off, he stood by helpless.

When I say I was done, I was *done*, done. He kept trying to call me for weeks. I would sometimes see his car sitting across the street from our house, but he didn't dare come to the door.

One of those times, I watched out the window as he sat in the car talking to himself until he got out and walked to the door. I closed the curtain and hopped onto the couch just as he rang the doorbell. I didn't budge.

Momma came stomping down the hallway "Girl, you hear that bell ringing?"

"Yeah."

"Why don't you answer it then? The hell wrong with you?"

"It's Samir."

"Oh. You stay right there. I got this."

I wasn't sure what Momma was gonna say when she opened that door, but I knew it wasn't going to be nothing nice.

Momma swung the door open, eyes narrowed. "What the hell you want?"

"Uh, hey, Momma J, is Toi here?" he asked timidly.

"Yeah, she here." The tone of her voice would have made *me* walk away. I held my breath as I sat on the couch listening. "As I said, what the hell you want? And don't Momma J me. It's Ms. Boxx to you."

"Yes, ma'am," he said, sounding sad. "Could I please talk to her?"

"Do you know how lucky you are that my baby needs me right now?" She spoke quietly, trying to stay calm. "You don't know how bad I want to hurt you. But I promised her I wouldn't do that because I don't need to be going to jail over yo' sorry ass. So, I'm going to say this one time and one time only. No, you can never talk to her again and don't come to my door nor call my phone no mo' or I'm going to have to break my promise." And she slammed the door in his face. She went straight down the hall to her room talking to herself. I didn't say anything because I knew better. She was super mad to be talking to herself.

I jumped up when I heard her bedroom door slam and looked out the window. He was standing on the porch still facing the door, head down and tears falling from his eyes. I can't lie, I felt bad for him and started crying myself. He looked up and saw me watching him and mouthed the words, "I'm sorry," and left. I didn't see him anymore after a while, which was fine with me. I moved on. He didn't come back to our school. It was what it was.

I was still miserable the rest of my junior year. It was a miracle I was able to keep my grades up. I was so heart broken. I kept my head down and avoided all the guys. I didn't date anyone. I was done with love. When my senior year started, I was feeling better but still just concentrated on graduating and enjoying my senior year. Until that summer.

Chapter 3

1995

Fresh out of high school, Kēssa and I decided to spend the summer kicking it. We went to the Montell Jordan/Total concert. My favorite/only/rich Auntie Renee came back for my graduation and took us traveling for a month to different historically black places—and ended the trip in Disney World in Orlando, Florida. When we came back, Auntie bought me a car. Kēssa and I went everywhere. As a matter of fact, the day I met LaMar we were on our way to a pool party David was throwing.

We knew all the fine guys were going to be there because that's all David hung out with, being a pretty boy himself with his Shamar Moore-looking ass. He was still trying to get with me, and I still couldn't do it.

Kēssa and I had to get extra cute and represent. Kēssa had on a black two-piece with yellow polka dots and some black jean shorts cut up basically to her crotch. My bathing suit was this shiny red material with tan shorts, and I was never seen without gold jewelry on. My hair was up in a cute bun on top of my head with my golden-brown highlights poppin'.

We were slowly driving down Military St. in the Village, bumping to EnVogue's "Don't Let Go," singing at the top of our lungs. Then I saw him. He was soooo fine, I slowed down even more.

Kēssa and I both were like, "DAMN!" sounding like Smokey and Craig on *Friday*.

You ever turn the music down to find a street? Well, I had to turn the music down to look at all that greatness! He walked outside, and that smile he flashed was brighter than the sun. He had dark chocolate skin, hair cut in a short fade, and a goatee highlighting those sexy-ass lips. He was wearing a Jordan jersey, white basketball shorts, and the new Air Jordan XIs that looked like they came fresh out the box. He wore diamond stud earrings in both ears and a thick silver chain, which complemented his skin tone. He looked to be six foot something. He reminded me of Morris Chestnut when he made his entrance on *The Best Man*.

I stopped suddenly and backed up. Glad no one was following close behind me because there would've been an accident for sure. Kēssa was sittin' there tryin' to push up whatever she could.

"Girl . . . wait . . . let me get myself together!"

I wasn't thinking about her. I was too busy praying he chose me. We had a deal that if we both liked the same guy—which with her seemed like all the time, but she swears she only likes light-skinned guys—the guy chooses. That way we don't step on each other's toes or break the sis code.

When I stopped, he and who I would later find out was his brother, came toward the car, squinting their eyes trying to see in.

I rolled the window down. "Excuse me. Does Kim live here?" I yelled across Kēssa out the passenger side window.

She looked at me like I was crazy and mouthed, "Who's Kim?"

"Naw, don't no females live here," both guys told us in unison as they walked up to the car.

"Oh, my bad," I said as I started to roll the window up.

"What you doing? They were coming over here!" Kēssa said, looking upset.

"Shhh, let me do this," I said, thinking, *This girl got no game.*

He knocked on the window, and I let it back down. "So you looking for someone named Kim for real?" he asked.

"Naw, I was making sure I didn't have to worry about your woman running up out that house."

"I was wondering who the hell Kim was," Kēssa added.

"First off, not my house. And second, I'm very single right now," he said, bringing a smile to my face.

Kēssa perked up then. "Well, in that case, I'm Kēssa and this is Toi." She waved over in my direction like I wasn't important.

"How you doing, Kēssa? Toi. I'm LaMar."

He was looking dead into my eyes when he flashed that smile again. All I could think was, *Choice made.*

"So, Toi, why you rolling through here with your music all loud, disturbing the peace?" he asked.

"How you going to be questioning me? You don't know me like that," I said with a little sass and a smile.

"So how do I get to know you like that then?"

His brother called him toward the back of my car and whispered something. Then he came back to my side and his brother went over to Kēssa's side. I could tell by the look on her face she wasn't happy that LaMar came over to me. But then she got a good look at his brother Malik and anyone with eyes could see he was just as fine and just her type, light-skinned, so she wasn't mad for long. She looked back at me and started cheesin' and shit.

LaMar leaned in. "As I was saying, Ms. Toi . . . how do I get to know you? Can I get your number or what?" I couldn't give him my number fast enough.

After meeting LaMar, we went ahead to the party, and it was the bomb! We had so much fun! David was all up in my face and the hate was real. I was getting dirty looks left and right. Not that I cared. I was allowing David to be all up on me to piss off the other females. I didn't want David before I met LaMar. No reason to change my mind. Still, it was fun to let them know I could have him if I wanted him. And I made sure to keep his attention on me all night.

"Why you dancing all on me like that?" David asked, smiling, as we walked into the house to get a drink.

"Because I want to." I smiled back.

"Word? You can dance all on me, but you can't be with me, huh?" He cornered me up against the counter, pressing his pelvis against me, leaning into my ear. His breath was cool against my skin, and I felt a little twitch where I shouldn't have. I looked over at him as his lips came toward mine.

"Boy, you know I don't have time for your ho-ish ways," I said and pushed him out my face before giving in.

THE NEXT DAY, KĒSSA AND I WERE AT MY HOUSE chillin', listening to music and laughing about all the hate we were receiving from the females and all the attention we were getting from the guys, when my phone rang. The Caller ID showed LaMar's name. I took my time answering.

"Oh my God, it's LaMar!" The butterflies were all through me. The phone kept ringing.

Kēssa shouted, "Answer the damn phone, fool! What are you doing?"

I answered the phone in the sexiest voice possible. "Hello."

"Hey, may I speak to Toi?"

"This is she. Who is this?" Like I didn't know.

"It's LaMar. How are you?"

I couldn't believe he was calling me already. Isn't there a rule of three days before calling or something like that?

"LaMar? LaMar who?" I said, playing crazy. Kēssa and I silently laughed as if I had just really done something.

"Oh dang! It's like that? You done forgot about me already? We met yesterday. You and your girl rolled up on us, music bumpin' . . . LaMar . . ."

"Oh yeah, the guy that likes to ask questions. How are you?" I asked, trying to hide the Kool-Aid smile in my voice.

"I'm great now that I hear your sexy voice. Dang! Do you always sound like that on the phone?"

"I don't know what you are talking about. This is just how I talk." I stuck my tongue out at Kēssa.

"Well, that voice def matches those looks. Just saying. But um, you almost made me forget why I was calling, sounding like that." I could hear the smile in his voice. "I was wondering when you would be free to hang out with me. You know, so I can get to know you enough to question you," he said, laughing.

"I don't know about all that, but I'm available whenever." I know I sounded way too available. I could've played a little hard to get.

"I'd like to take you out tonight to chill and talk. What do you like to do?" This was way before Netflix and Chill.

"Surprise me. I want to see how you roll." Kēssa and I gave each other a silent high-five.

"Okay. I can do that. Can we hook up at, let's say . . . eight thirty?"

"That's cool with me."

"You don't have to get dressed up or anything like that. I got just the place."

"I hope it's not the same place you take all your other females. I'm special."

"Yes, you are special, and I don't have any other females. And no, I haven't taken anyone there. Just found the spot myself the other day. So where do I pick you up at?"

I gave him my address and we hung up. When I tell you I got off that phone juiced (that means excited), I mean I was juiced! I looked at Kēssa and we both just fell out with excitement.

KĒSSA HELPED ME PICK OUT WHAT TO WEAR. I DIDN'T want him to think I was trying too hard; nonetheless, I had to look bomb when he showed up. I wanted him to watch me walk out and think, *That's wifey right there*. After trying on this and that we finally settled on me wearing my red FUBU V-neck shirt and dark blue Guess shorts with red-and-gold sandals. I wore my hair down and flat ironed it straight. I had it cut like Aaliyah's. You know I had to rock my bamboo earrings. I was so ready!

When he pulled up, he got out of the car to come to the door, but I was already on my way out. I needed him to see me walk out with my hair flowing in the wind. He went toward the passenger side door of his dark blue IROC –Z Camaro, then looked up and saw me. He stopped in his tracks and his mouth fell open. I smiled and waved, which seemed to take him out of his temporary trance. He opened the car door to let me get in and ran around to his side.

He couldn't get in fast enough. He was fumbling with the door and keys. He was excited, and I liked the way it made me feel.

He finally pulled himself together. "You look amazing! I got stuck for a minute." He gave me a nervous smile.

"Thank you. You're looking quite handsome yourself." He had on a Bulls T-shirt and some black jean shorts. "I take it you like the Bulls?" I said, trying to make small talk.

"Yeah, Jordan my boy. I play ball too. Maybe you'll come watch me play one day." He was already trying to sneak in another date.

"Where are we going?"

"You'll see."

He took me to a little hidden spot out at Lake Hefner. He got out of the car and went to the trunk, walked about halfway into the field, and set down a picnic basket. He then laid out a large blanket, set out a CD player, took out glasses and wine, and started tossing rose petals all around. When he was done, he came and got me out the car and we walked over. I remember it being completely green all around us and there being a nice breeze. The conditions were perfect.

We took off our shoes and sat down, and he began playing music. We laughed and discovered that we had a lot in common as we listened to Gerald Levert, Boyz II Men, Jodeci, etc. We found that we liked the same music, food, actors, and movies. Just simple things. He laid out fresh fruit, potato salad, and fried chicken. All he made himself. The wine he brought was Moscato, which I had never had before.

After eating, he fired up a blunt and offered it to me. I hadn't smoked before either, but I didn't want to seem like a square, so I went ahead and hit it a couple of times. I was feeling good and comfortable with him. Then his favorite song, "Before You Turn Off the Lights," an old song by W.C. W. C. with Michel'le came on. He took me by the hand and pulled me up to slow dance. He made me feel special. He didn't even try to feel on my booty, which made me like him more. He was the perfect gentleman. I should've known then I was meeting the representative.

For the next several months, we were on the phone every night. And every chance we got we would hang out at his house or mine—as long as my momma wasn't home. He would come up with something cute to do like going to the park or walking around downtown. I didn't notice he spent very little money. If we stopped somewhere to eat, that was the only time he bought anything.

His favorite thing to do was to go out to Woodson gym and play basketball. He still dreamed of being a ballplayer and he definitely had skills.

The first time he took me there, he was so proud when he walked in with me.

"Six-six, that you?" one of the guys asked, nodding toward me.

"Fo' sho," he said, beaming.

I sat in the stands and cheered for this man like he was on an NBA team and would receive millions of dollars for the work he put in. Hell, he was playing like that too. It was obvious he was showing out for me, and I loved it.

After, we were sitting in the car waiting for the air conditioner to cool.

"That was fun!" I was still feeling the rush of watching him.

"I heard you cheering me on. That's what's up."

"I mean, I couldn't help but to acknowledge yo' skills," I said, shooting a fake shot.

He rolled his head toward me. "Yeah. It felt good having you here. I got a question fo' you though."

"Okay."

"How you feel about me claiming you like that?"

"Huh? You talkin' about when we walked in?"

"Yeah."

"I mean, I didn't have a problem with it."

He reached over and held my hand. "So, you ready to be my lady?" he asked with a sexy look on his face.

"Yes." I answered calmly but was flippin' out on the inside.

"Cool," he said, nodding. He looked away and quickly looked back. "Hey . . ."

I turned to look at him and he stared into my eyes.

"I love you."

"I love you, too," I replied, and he leaned over and kissed me.

I imagined plenty of times how that would be said, and I always figured I'd be the first to say it. It meant so much more that he said it first.

As soon as I got home, I called Kēssa over.

"What is the emergency?" she asked, flopping down on my bed.

"Girl, you not gone believe this!" I was about to bust out my skin with excitement.

"You look crazy. What is it? Did you and LaMar do it or something?"

"No. He asked me to be his lady and told me he loved me!"

Now, I thought my best friend would match my energy, but I didn't get the reaction I was expecting.

"He said that before y'all did it or after?"

I stopped jumping around long enough to look at her. The look on her face wasn't of joy.

"I told you we didn't do it. What's wrong with you?"

"Malik and I did it and then he broke up with me. I assumed since they brothers, they both did the same thing." She started to cry.

"Awww, Kēss, I'm sorry." I hugged her. "I'm gone beat his ass. Don't even worry about it."

"You always get the good ones."

I didn't say anything to that. In this case, she wasn't wrong. I later found out she lied. But that's another story for another day.

THE FIRST TIME WE MADE LOVE WAS LIKE A MOVIE scene. At least to me it was. It was sometime after midnight, and we were in one of our hidden chill spots, sitting in the car listening to music and smoking. I was playing a game of "keep the blunt away" with him when he suddenly stopped and just stared at me.

"Why are you looking at me like that?" I asked.

"You're so beautiful. Sometimes I can't believe I'm with you."

That was it for me. I was completely turned on and knew right then I was going to give him some. No one had ever called me beautiful. Sexy or fine, but never beautiful. The fact that my dad passed when I was a baby and I never got to hear that from him made me subconsciously thirsty to hear it. And when LaMar said it, something changed in me.

I wasn't even nervous. Now remember, I had only been with one other guy, and I didn't really enjoy it. It didn't feel special. But I knew somehow this would be different.

I hitched up my sundress and climbed over the armrest into his lap. He clumsily put the seat back, and it gave a loud pop and a jerk. He looked a it embarrassed for a moment. We started kissing and grinding, then he reached between my legs and slid his fingers inside me.

"Damn, you wet," he whispered. "You sure you're ready for this?"

"Yes," I responded as I reached into his basketball shorts, pulled his dick out, and started stroking it. I lifted up, and he held my panties to the side. I took a deep breath and slid him inside me. He and I both moaned at the same time. Things from there were like in slow motion. I don't know when he got my breasts out, but he kept saying how pretty they were while he was putting them in his mouth. He took his time. Kissed me and touched me just right. All the while H-Town's "Knocking da Boots" was playing on repeat.

That was the first time I felt like I had made love. Afterward, we talked and held hands as we discussed what happened. Somewhere during that conversation, I asked him about his ex. This was when my Tina Turner syndrome developed. You're probably wondering what that is. Well, think back to the movie *What's Love Got to Do with It*. The part where Ike came back from the hospital after his girl had shot herself. When he was talking about all the people he helped and how they left him, Tina told him, "I wouldn't do that . . . what those other people did to you, leave you. I would never do that." She meant that shit and so did I when I basically said the same thing.

He told me that they broke up when she moved to New York. He didn't go with her because he had recently found his birth family, and he was still getting to know them. So he woke up one morning and she was gone. He never heard from her again. The sadness in his eyes touched me deeply. I hurt for him. Then he looked at me, smiled, and said, "Now, I have you. But I'm scared. I don't want to lose you." And guess what I said. Tina Turner syndrome.

~

WE HAD BEEN TOGETHER FOR MONTHS, SO I FIGURED IT was finally time to introduce him to my mother. She wasn't happy

I had fallen for him so hard after the heartbreak I went through with Samir. It's hard to forget when your child goes through that much pain. But since I was so smitten, she had to meet him.

I warned LaMar that she might be a little hard on him, so he was prepared. We waited in the living room what seemed like forever after I told her he was there. When she finally came out, LaMar jumped up and offered his hand. "Hello, Mrs. Boxx."

"That's Ms. Boxx," she corrected, ignoring his hand with "the look" on her face. She looked him up and down.

We all stood there staring at each other. That look was stronger than I've ever seen before and had me wondering what I may have done wrong before bringing him over. And it wasn't who she was naturally. She's a small lady—around five foot six, medium build. She has jet-black hair, dark eyes, high cheekbones with red-toned skin. She is so pretty that you wouldn't think she could ever look mean. But she knew how to work that face.

"So, you're LaMar, huh?" she finally asked, sucking her teeth.

"Yes, ma'am," LaMar answered and flashed his smile.

"Why you smiling so hard? You special or somethin'?"

"Ummm, no, ma'am."

"You can sit."

"Yes, ma'am." He sat down quickly. Hell, she had the face going so hard, I was scared to look her in the eye.

"I'm just going to let you know up front . . . I don't trust you as far as I can throw you, but I'm going to give you a chance because I know it's important to her." Momma nodded toward me. "But know, I will go to jail or hell for mine. You got that?"

"Yes, ma'am," LaMar replied and swallowed hard.

Over dinner she asked him a ton of questions on what his intentions were and what he was going to do with his future. His answers even impressed me. He was extremely charismatic and won her over. She pulled out the dominos and he let her win a few games. He was so proud of himself when he left. And he should've been because she was determined not to like him. I, on the other hand, felt a slight bit of déjà vu. Samir, too, was able to win her over with his charms. She loved that boy like a son. I started to realize she was more like a spider with no venom. She just looked scary.

They got along so well, she even let him call her Momma Jewel. Everyone else had to call her Momma J. Which proved he really was special. She'd call me and ask for him. He'd go over and fix something for her or help her pull weeds or cut her grass or clean her gutters. I didn't know if he was a servant or her son-in-law. But he loved every minute of it. Eventually she just started calling him directly. The first time it happened messed me up. We were on the couch at Malik's watching a movie. He answered the phone, and I could hear a female's voice and his side of the conversation.

"Mmm-hmm," he said, pushing me off him. "Oh, that's gotta be taken care of." He got off the couch, walked to the back, and returned with his shoes in hand. "Oh, we weren't doing nothing important."

I watched him move about, wondering, *Who the hell is that?*

He slid his feet into his shoes. "Okay, I'm on my way!"

"Who was that?"

"Momma Jewel. She needs me to come by the house right quick."

"Wait. When my momma start calling you directly?"

"When I gave her my number. She shouldn't have to bother you if she lookin' for me."

"Weren't you just over there yesterday? It couldn't wait till we finish this movie?"

"It's on tape. We can watch it anytime. I'll be right back," he said, kissing my forehead and leaving me just sitting there looking crazy.

But I was happy that they were getting along.

Chapter 4

1996-1998

Things were going so well that LaMar and I got an apartment together. We had decent jobs. Mine was due to my wonderful Auntie Renee. She used her connections and hooked me and Kēssa up with good-paying jobs at an ad agency. Though we didn't go to college, they set us up with a program to help get the certifications we needed. I loved the job, but Kēssa only lasted three weeks, talking about they were doing too much. But I saw an opportunity to become a project manager and that was my goal. I was willing to do what was needed to get to that level.

LaMar was working as a grill chef in an expensive restaurant. He loved cooking and claimed to want to become a chef someday. He made decent money, and I was proud of him.

Things were perfect. Since he got home first, he would cook dinner and keep the house clean—or should I say his OCD kept the house clean. When I got home, he would do little things like rub my feet or my back, run me baths. And for the next six months, we made love, laughed, and took care of each other. He became my lover and best friend. I thought I'd never feel love again. But he made it easy to love and trust him.

~

It was Christmas morning when I found out I was pregnant with our first child. I was so scared to tell him. He had just lost his job a few days before I found out, so it wasn't good timing. But when is it ever good timing to get pregnant unless you're rich?

I had to tell him and Momma at the same time, so after visiting his family we went over to Momma's to eat and exchange gifts. I figured that would be the best time of any to spring it on them. I put the pregnancy test in a box and wrapped it for LaMar to open.

"Man, I'm so full," LaMar said, flopping down on the couch, rubbing his stomach. "Momma Jewel, you did that."

"I know and stop flopping down on my furniture."

"Sorry. I felt too heavy to sit."

"I'm ready to open my gift. Where's it at?" Momma said, holding out her hands.

I handed her a long box and LaMar one as well.

"Baby, what's this? I thought we opened all ours this morning," he asked, smiling.

"I wanted you to open that one here."

"Momma Jewel, you go first," LaMar said.

Momma tore into hers.

"Ohhhh, this is beautiful, baby. I love it!" she said, looking at the diamond tennis bracelet I gave her. LaMar leaned forward and helped her put it on.

"I knew you'd love that, Momma Jewel. You like to get yo' bling on," LaMar said, like he bought it.

"Okay, LaMar, open yours," I told him.

LaMar slowly unwrapped the box. My stomach was in knots. I didn't know how either of them was going to feel. I hoped I wasn't ruining Christmas.

He opened the box and looked at it in confusion. "I don't get it . . ."

"What is it?" Momma asked, stretching her neck.

LaMar picked it up and looked at it closely.

"Does this mean what I think it means?" he asked, his eyes wide.

"Yeah." My heart was beating so hard, I felt it in my throat.

"What is it? What it mean?" Momma asked. LaMar turned it toward Momma.

"That's a pregnancy test, ain't it?" She looked confused for a minute. "Wait . . . are you . . ."

"Pregnant. Yes."

Her mouth fell open.

We both looked at LaMar. He was still in the same position, holding the test. He was so still I had to watch his stomach to make sure he was breathing, as if the news had turned him to stone.

"Well? Are we happy? Sad? What?" I asked.

LaMar finally looked at me, walked over, pulled me up into his arms, and started to cry.

"This is the best gift I've ever had," he said, hugging me tightly.

"Really? You're happy?"

"I'm so happy."

Momma came over and joined the hug.

"Awww, my babies are having me a baby!" she cried.

When I told Kēssa, she was happy too, since she had Ke'Sari the year before.

"It's about time y'all had one. Now I won't be the only one walking around with a baby."

We were all excited. At first, he felt guilty that he wasn't working, but he made up for it by catering to me constantly. And the bigger I got, the more he did. He even washed my hair and painted my toenails. I felt like a queen.

A month before I had the baby, Momma and Kēssa threw me a baby shower. We got all that we needed and then some.

We welcomed our first son, LaMar Jr. (LJ) in September of 1996.

That was a crazy day. I was having contractions but was only dilated to a two, according to the doctor who sent me back home to suffer. My back was killing me. I was hot and sick of being pregnant. We were at Momma's, and I was complaining about what I was feeling.

"Why you sittin' over there whining? You should be out walking."

"What's walking going to do, Momma?"

"It's gone make that baby come out."

"The doctor told me to stimulate her nipples and for us to have sex more," LaMar said.

"That shit don't work. That's how you get 'em in there, not how you get 'em out. You gotta walk 'em down."

"I'll trying anything," I said, struggling to get up.

LaMar came and gave me a hand. "You 'bout to do it right now? You want me to go?"

"No, I'm just going to turn a few corners."

"You shouldn't go by yo' self," Momma stated, drying her hands on a towel.

"I'll be fine." I didn't believe it would change anything anyway.

Boy, was I wrong. I couldn't even make it back. The labor pains hit me so hard, I had to sit on the curb a few times. I was sitting in somebody's yard when Momma and LaMar found me.

"Girl, what are you doing?" She parked the car and hopped out.

"Sitting here in pain."

"Baby, you scared us. You've been gone for almost an hour," LaMar said as he and Momma pulled me up off the ground. "I knew I should've come with you."

They helped me into the car.

"Do you think you need to go to the hospital? How close are the contractions?"

"I don't know, Momma. Let's just go back to the house."

I stretched out on the couch. LaMar pulled up a chair and sat directly in front of me, right in my face, watching his watch. Every time I would wince, he'd ask, "Was that a contraction?"

After about the fifteenth of those, he was on my nerves.

"Was that a contraction?"

"Boy, get out my face and leave me alone! And let go of my damn hand. And quit breathing on me! You making me hot!"

"Stop hollering at that boy. He just making sure you're okay," Momma fussed at me.

It got late and we all ended up falling asleep. I woke up in severe pain around one thirty in the morning. All the noise I made woke up LaMar, and he was right back in my face.

After three hours of him timing me, the pain had become more consistent. I tried to hide it, but still LaMar was watching me like a hawk. I don't know why but I really didn't want to go to the hospital.

LaMar knocked on Momma's bedroom door. "Momma Jewel, I think we need to get her to the hospital now."

Momma comes out tying her robe, yawning. "You ready to go, baby?"

"No, I'm good."

"Her contractions have been three to four minutes apart for the last couple of hours."

As soon as he said that, I had another one.

"It's not time yet. Momma, tell him it's not time." I tried to do Lamaze breathing like I'd seen on TV.

Momma flipped on the light and looked at me. "Girl, get yo' ass up and let's go! You not gone have that baby on my damn couch."

They got me in the car and as we were on our way to the hospital, the contractions hit me harder. Momma was driving the speed limit and stopping at every light like we were out for a leisurely ride.

"Momma, could you please just run the light?"

"I'm not no damn emergency vehicle. You not about to have me in no accident."

I looked around and there were literally no cars out.

I was so happy when we got to the hospital and into my room. It was a big room with a couch and recliner. And after I got my epidural, I was able to watch TV and relax. Momma and LaMar both fell asleep on the couch. Around eight a.m., everything speeded up when the nurse checked me and felt the baby's head.

LaMar held my hand through the whole thing and with about seven pushes, LJ was born.

When LaMar held him for the first time, he cried. Which made me and Momma cry. It was the sweetest thing I've ever seen.

Momma finally got her hands on him.

"He looks just like you, LaMar. He's so handsome."

"Yeah, he's definitely a junior. I don't need no test to confirm it either."

"You sholl don't. Couldn't deny 'im if you tried." Momma looked at LaMar out the corner of her eye. "I just hope he has his momma's drive and commitment." Momma laughed.

"That's messed up, Momma Jewel." LaMar obviously felt hurt.

"I'm just saying I hope he can keep a job like his momma. Anyways, just so y'all know, I'm not about to be nobody's Grandma. Y'all gone have to come up with something better than that," she said, smiling at LJ.

"Like what, Momma Jewel?" LaMar asked.

"Hell, I don't know, but I'm too young and fabulous to be called Grandma, NaNa, or MawMaw." Then she looked at LJ and said, "Ain't that right, baby? I'm too cute for that shit. Yes, I am."

I didn't know anything other than the names she called out and said she didn't want, so I called Auntie. Even then she was living out of the country somewhere ,so she should know something. I put her on speaker.

"Congratulations on the baby. I hate I'm not there to see him. My first great-nephew. Who the baby look like?" Auntie asked.

"Just like his bighead daddy," Momma answered.

"What y'all name him?"

"LaMar Junior." LaMar spoke proudly.

"Oh," was all she said.

"Auntie, we're trying to come up with something more unique for LJ to call Momma. You got any ideas?"

"Yeah, he can call her ass Grandma," Auntie replied, laughing.

"The hell he can!" Momma shouted back.

"How about Granny?"

"Bitch, don't make me hang up this phone!"

"Stop cussin' in front of that baby."

"He don't even understand what words are yet. I can cuss."

"Okay, how about *abuela*? That's Spanish for grandma," she suggested.

"Do I look like I speak-a Spanish to you?" Momma replied.

"You should. We lived in Mexico a couple of years when we were little. You remember that."

"I do and I didn't speak-a Spanish then either. I don't even look like no damn *abuela*."

"You kinda do look like you got a little Mexican in you. Especially around the eyes and nose," LaMar said.

"Shut up, boy. What else you got?"

"How about *oma*?"

"That sounds just like grandma. Nope. Next."

"Ummm, well when I was in the Philippines, they used Lola."

"Lola. Lola. Hmm. I kinda like that. Sound exotic. Okay. Lola it is."

LaMar's family came by. His dad and big brother were happy for us.

"'Bout time you had one, bro. Shoot, I have three already."

"That's because you a hoe."

"Fuck you."

"He's a handsome one, son."

His adopted mother Della came. His real mother passed a few months after he was born, so she's the only mother he's ever had. That woman didn't seem to like anyone. Not his real dad and not me either. She barely spoke to any of us when she walked in. She had a scowl on her face when she looked at each of us and didn't smile till she saw her son.

LaMar jumped up and hugged her. "Hey, Ma. You know Dad, Malik, and Toi. This is Momma Jewel. She's Toi Momma."

"Mm-hmm. Hey. Nice to meet you." You could tell by her tone, she didn't mean it.

Momma sucked her teeth. "Mm-hmm. You too."

"You can't speak, Della?" Mr. Greg asked.

She simply looked at him and waved. He laughed to himself and shook his head.

"Can I see the baby?"

LaMar hurried over and gently picked up LJ and walked him proudly over to his mother and placed him into her arms.

She stared at him. "Mm-hmm."

"Isn't he handsome, Momma? Looks just like me, huh?"

"I guess so."

Momma looked at me and mouthed, "What the hell wrong with her?"

I shrugged.

Everyone left to give us time to rest, but a few hours later Kēssa and her little girl Ke'Sari showed up.

She went straight to LJ and picked him up. "Sis, he is so handsome. He looks like LaMar."

"Everyone is sayin' that."

"LaMar, why didn't one of y'all call me so I could be here? That's just all kinds of wrong."

"We were just trying to get here. Your sister acted like she didn't even want to have the baby in the hospital," LaMar explained.

"Girl, I was scared. I didn't think to call nobody."

"I'm still mad at y'all. Somebody should've thought of me."

Good ole Kēssa, making things about her.

ONCE WE WERE HOME, LaMar WAS WONDERFUL WITH both of us. He was the one who got up with LJ whenever he would wake in the middle of the night. He had no issues changing his diapers, even the poopy ones. He even went out and bought a breast pump so he could have bottles to feed him. He was a good dad who ended up turning into a stay-at-home dad. After my six weeks, I went back to work. But I wasn't worried about him not working because I didn't want to put our baby in daycare. I could manage the bills. Also, if I needed anything, my Momma and Auntie had our backs and sometimes his dad would help out. We were living well. Not a lot of stress or worries. It was all good.

SKIPPING FORWARD, LJ WAS ALMOST TWO, AND I FOUND out I was pregnant again. LaMar was more excited than I was about having another baby. I wasn't ready. My career was taking off. I'd started taking the classes needed to prepare myself for the project manager position and only had a month to go when I found out. What worried me was the sickness. I was so sick with LJ. I couldn't take off a bunch of sick days right after I moved into a new position. I prayed that it would be better this time. And that taking maternity leave didn't disrupt my promo-tion. I didn't want the higher-ups thinking I was unreliable, wondering when I'd pop another kid out.

LaMar got another job working in a nice restaurant and things were great. I finally had some help with the household income. He paid his bills. I paid mine. I was able to save a good amount of money since I wasn't paying for every expense. LJ was in a good daycare we trusted. LaMar was able to work his shift, pick up LJ, and still have dinner ready when I got home.

One day I came home, and he had cooked one of my favorite meals. Me being a Taurus, I considered that part of my love language. He knew that and always found a way to use it to his advantage.

I went into the bedroom and got comfortable. When I came out, he was setting the table.

"Hey, beautiful. How was your day?" He looked over at me and smiled. I still loved that smile.

"It was long. They gave me a couple of special projects to do. I killed it of course. Max came to my desk and said I did things he didn't even consider doing." I pretended to pop my collar. "It's all a matter of time before I'm working with him as his colleague instead of his employee."

"That's what's up. My baby gone be running thangs in a minute. Come have a seat right here with yo' smart ass." He pulled out my chair.

"Where's my baby?" I asked, sitting down.

"Momma Jewel came and snatched him up." He hurried into the kitchen and brought out two plates. He put them down and took his seat.

I looked at the food. "This is different. It's been a long time since you and I sat down and had dinner together. What's the occasion?"

"No occasion. Just wanted to show you some love." He leaned over and kissed me.

"Well, I appreciate the love."

"Oh shit! I forgot the music."

He turned on some slow jams and continued to ask me more about my day. He told me a funny story about something cute LJ did when Momma came and picked him up, and we laughed and ate.

Just before we finished eating, he said, "So, umm, I do have something I need to tell you." He didn't even look at me.

I immediately lost my appetite. I put my fork down and looked at him. He just kept looking at his plate, pushing his broccoli around.

"What is it, LaMar?"

"Don't get mad, okay?" He glanced up at me and quickly shifted his eyes back down.

"Don't tell me how to respond before I know what I'm responding to. I'm going to feel how I feel according to what comes out of yo' mouth."

"I know, but just don't get mad, okay?"

"You saying that is making me mad."

"Man—"

"What is it, LaMar!"

"I got fired today but it wasn't my fault." He blurted it out so fast I almost didn't hear him.

"Did you say you got fired?"

"Yeah."

"Why? What happened?"

He just sat there shaking his head, still playing with his food.

"LaMar, look at me." He put his fork down and looked at me. "What happened?"

"My boss be trippin'. I was a few minutes late a couple of times. Traffic happened, really. He didn't want to hear that, so he let me go."

My heart dropped a little. All I could think was, *Not again.* The timing was hella bad. Here I was about to give birth to our second child and would have to carry the family again. It took everything in me not to blow up on him.

"I'm sorry, baby." He looked at me with such sadness in his eyes. "I don't mean to be a burden on you."

I walked over and placed his head to my bosom. "Baby, don't even trip. We're straight. This is why I was saving." I lifted his face and looked into his eyes. "You'll get another job. Hopefully one you like. I'm not even worried about it."

He stood up and looked down at me. "You the bomb! I love

you so much." And then he kissed me and took me into the bedroom and did things to me I didn't know we could do while I was pregnant.

I gave birth to our second son in June of 1998. We named him Tyree Myzel. And like before, LaMar worked as a stay-at-home dad. And he was great at it. I knew home was taken care of. So it was all good.

Chapter 5

Upward

Believe it or not, I enjoyed going to work. I liked handling projects. I liked the praise from my supervisors. Part of me even liked supporting my family. I finished those classes and was just waiting for the day to come when my manager, Max, would let me know I'd been selected. I made sure to dress for the position I wanted instead of the one I was in. I walked up in there every day with a bright smile on my face and all positive energy. So much so, everyone started calling me Sunshine.

I remember the day that I got promoted like it was yesterday. I got called into managers' meetings all the time. It was kinda like an intern-type thing, so when they called me in that day, it wasn't a surprise.

Max went over his usual stats. It was exciting to me at the time but none of the actual managers seemed to like it. Midway through the meeting, Max asked Cadena to come and talk about some other things that was going on within the company. I watched her as she walked to the front. She's tall like me, a little bit thicker and a tad bit darker. Her big, black, curly wig bounced along the way. Shoulders back and back straight, she walked with grace in her grey pantsuit. Her presence demanded attention. She usually led our team meetings, but she very seldom spoke in any of the manager meetings unless she was correcting Max about something. She held her own as the only black woman in her position. And you could tell she- took pride in her work. I actually admired her even though my coworker, Dwayne, and I talked about her under our breath in every meeting she had with us. She was always cheerful, put together, and she seemed to know more about the company than any of her male counterparts. I watched her speak, in awe, and couldn't wait till it was my turn to do what she did. If that time ever came. It had been over a year since I passed all the classes with flying colors and started being the person they brought all the extra work to without the extra money that goes along with it. Hell, I probably knew more than most the managers up in there, too.

At the end of the meeting, she made an announcement.

"Before we go, I have one more important thing to go over. It's not often that I get to do this, but I requested this privilege. Toi, could you join me, please." Cadena waved me over.

I immediately got nervous. They usually didn't acknowledge me in any way. I always sat in the back and just listened and took notes. I got up and slowly walked to where she stood in front of everyone. It was weird looking out at all the faces looking back at me. Some of the men were stern-faced, some had smiles.

"Toi, it hasn't gone unnoticed that you're a hard worker. You've come up with some great ideas on how we can change things for the better. You're always here and eager to learn new things and when given a special project you go above and beyond our expectations. So, it's a great honor for me to give you the keys to your very own office." She brought her hand from behind her back and dangled the keys in front of me. I held out my hand and she dropped them into it. "Congratulations. You're now one of us."

They all began to clap. I was so excited I hugged the poor lady.

"Sorry. Thank you! Thank you all so much!"

"No, thank you. You deserve it."

We all filed out of the meeting, each person congratulating me personally on the way out. Cadena then walked me over to my new office. It was centrally located right off the elevator. I unlocked the door and slowly swung it open. Inside was a huge desk and tons of space. I couldn't help but smile from ear to ear.

"Why don't you take a seat behind your new desk?" she suggested.

I walked over and sat. The chair felt as though it was waiting for me.

"I'll give you a minute to take this all in. From one black woman to another, I'm very proud of you. We had three others to choose from, all men, and your contributions outweighed them all." She smiled before leaving and closing the door behind her.

I sat there a minute and took a spin in my chair. I pretended to have someone sitting in front of me, giving them instructions. Being in there made me feel like a boss. The excitement overwhelmed me. I stood up and walked around, figuring out where I would place pictures of my kids and mom. I saw where I would want a couple of plants. I opened the shades to the big window behind my desk. Wasn't a fantastic view, but I could see the big trees on the other side of the parking lot. I opened the shades for the big side window, and across the hall I could see into another office. The guy in there was handsome. I had seen him around plenty but wasn't sure what his name was. He worked for another department, so I would probably only see him in passing. All I knew was, if his shades were open, mine would be too. That was a better view than the one I had outside.

Cadena walked back in while I was staring across the hall and startled me.

"I was thinking we could sit down together and come up with some talking points that you'll want to go over when you're introduced to your team tomorrow."

"Okay. Thank you."

She walked over to me. "That's Craven. Don't know anything about him other than he's polite, he dresses nice, and he isn't too bad on the eyes. I've always wanted this office just because he's part of the view. Don't tell anyone I said that."

"I won't."

I RUSHED HOME AFTER WORK TO LET MY MAN KNOW I finally made it to the project management position. He was so happy for me that he picked me up and spun me around.

"All yo' hard work finally paid off! What now?"

"Now I won't have to work as hard. I can have other people do it," I said, and we laughed.

"I'm so proud of you, babe. We gotta celebrate. I'm going to call Momma Jewel."

We met up with Momma, Kēssa, and the girls at Spaghetti Warehouse and celebrated. Momma paid for my meal. I paid for everybody else's.

Kēssa was broke taking care of now two babies, living paycheck to paycheck. I told her she should've stayed up there with me. LaMar had saved up a little money, but I think he spent most of that on gas and weed.

But I didn't let any of that ruin my moment.

THE NEXT DAY I KNEW EXACTLY WHAT I WAS GOING TO say and how I was going to present myself to my team. I wasn't nervous at all because I had been practicing for this day for so long. I had a clear plan and direction on what I expected. They were a well-established team and good at what they did. I was thankful it wasn't a bunch of newbies.

That morning I woke up early. I actually had trouble sleeping I was so excited. I had the perfect pantsuit I'd set aside for this very day—red and pinstriped. I worked hard after having Ty to get my body back, and that blazer fit my curves perfectly. I would say my look was sex-fessional. That's sexy and professional.

I walked into work with my head held high. I decided to take the stairs, I was feeling so good. Craven and I reached the door at the same time.

"Good morning." He smiled and opened the door for me. "Ladies first."

"Thank you."

Now, y'all know there are three things that I love about a man. Muscular arms, which I could see he had even through his dress shirt, pretty eyes, and a beautiful smile. His smile touched me in private places. That's all I got to say about that.

As I was walking ahead of him, I felt his eyes on me but maybe that was just wishful thinking.

He hurried to open the door when we reached our landing. "Have a wonderful day."

"You too." I stopped at my door and watched him walk into his office.

What a start to my day! I enjoyed putting my key in the lock and opening my door. I hurried and opened the blinds to the side window just as Craven was doing the same, and he smiled at me again.

I pulled out the pictures of my kids, my mom, and one of me and LaMar and arranged them on my desk.

I sat in my tall, comfortable, wonderful chair and took another spin before turning on my computer to read my emails.

Someone knocked on my door.

"Enter," I said, and even that felt good.

Cadena came in with a smile. "I see you're getting settled. May I?" She picked up and looked at my pictures. "Who are these two cute little people?"

"The big one is LJ and the little one is Ty."

"They're adorable." She set that picture down and picked up the one of me and LaMar. "You're married?"

"No, ma'am. That's their dad LaMar."

She nodded and put the picture back onto my desk.

"You ready for this meet-and-greet?"

"Yes, ma'am!" I said standing.

"Wow! You look amazing!"

"Thank you."

I felt fully confident when we walked into the conference room. I also felt all eyes on me as we both walked to the front of the room.

"Good morning, everyone," she said loudly to get their attention.

"Good morning," they all said in unison and not with a lot of enthusiasm.

Cadena introduced me. I stood and smiled. I could see a few females look at me up and down and the guys smiled. A lot.

"I'm going to leave you guys in Toi's more-than-capable hands," Cadena said and walked toward the door. Before she walked out and closed it, she turned back. "Let me know if you need me to come back in here." She looked at each person as if she was leaving me in a room full of high schoolers instead of adults.

"Good morning. As you've already heard my name is Toi," I said.

I gave them a short rendition of how I came to be where I am and about my family. The only person who really asked any questions was this guy named Ricky. It was obvious he had thoughts on moving up, and I let him know I would help him any way I could.

I then took out a soccer ball that I had written questions on. I told them to toss it to each other and answer the question their thumb landed on. It was a great icebreaker, a different way to introduce ourselves, and turned out to be really fun.

FOR THE NEXT FEW WEEKS, I MADE SURE THAT WHEN I got to work, I would personally speak to each agent and answer any questions. I wanted them to know that I was down to earth and approachable. I even had a team lunch in the conference room with them one day and brought in barbecue with all the sides, not just some ol' boring pizza. That hour helped me to really learn the different personalities. Ricky made sure to sit by me, and we got a chance to talk about a few different things. He's funny and intelligent. So much so he's taught himself how to speak different languages.

I had one-on-ones with each agent as well.

The last one was Ricky.

He peeked his head through the door. "You ready for me?"

"Yes." I gestured for him to take a seat.

He was a handsome man. Around six foot one, with mocha-colored skin. He's a good thick, not fat. Nice eyes and smile. The only thing I didn't really like is that he wore braids. But he dressed nice.

"You look nice today," he said.

"Thank you. Are there any questions you have for me?"

"Yeah, but I don't think it's appropriate to ask yo' boss those types of questions." He laughed.

"Ha, ha. Very funny. No seriously."

He asked questions about the internship and classes. I gave him the full rundown. Even offered to walk him through how to apply.

We were in there for a couple of hours, and it was well past lunch when my stomach growled loudly.

"I'm so sorry. I've took up all yo' time."

"Oh, you heard that," I said, embarrassed.

"Yeah. Are you allowed to have lunch with your employees?"

"I don't think that's a good idea. Don't want people thinking there's going to be some kind of quid pro quo thing going on around here." I got an email flagged as important. "Give me a sec." I read it—and it said he was transferring under another manager. "Oh, so I guess you don't like me. I see you transferred."

"Nothing against you, and I hope you won't take offense. It's just hard to work under someone you want to work under. Your beauty distracts me."

"You're kidding, right?"

"Partly. No, for real I wasn't supposed to be on this side of things initially. I came in a few weeks ago and was just waiting for someone to transition out. Plus, they wanted me to learn the entry level of things over here. That way when I'm team leader over there people who have been here a while won't feel uncomfortable. Some of them are already upset that I came in off the street."

"So, this whole time you've been infiltrating my territory? You're an impostor."

"Something like that. I appreciate everything I've learned from you though. And I'm still going to take those classes you were telling me about. So again, I know I'm not quite on your level just yet, but you wanna go grab something to eat?"

I laughed and grabbed my purse.

Chapter 6

Is It All Good

Even though I was thriving at work, things at home seemed different. I mean, we used to do family stuff together every week. We would take the boys to Lake Hefner on the weekends or go to LJ's favorite place, Chuck E. Cheese. They weren't old enough to do much else. We'd have Kēssa or Malik meet us with their kids so the boys could play with their cousins. We'd go over to Momma's on Sundays and have dinner. LaMar and I would catch a movie or go chill at our old hangout by the lake.

Sex was always plentiful, though we usually had to wait till the boys were asleep. Then we'd rip each other's clothes off. I couldn't keep his hands off me, and I decided to get the depo shot because I had a feeling he was trying to put another baby in me.

But all that had kinda stopped. He was doing his thing and I mine. I would take the kids somewhere, and he'd go over to his dad's or Malik's. I guess having two little people to keep up with was taking its toll on us. During that time, most nights we'd give each other a quick kiss and pass out. I didn't mind it, but it was starting to put a little distance between us.

Soon, we were looking to rent a house. He would be so excited when he'd find a nice house with a rental sign.

"Babe, I bet we could afford this house! It looks nice, too!" he said as soon as I answered the phone.

"For real? Where's it at?"

"Two blocks from Pop's house."

"I don't know if I want to stay over there though. There's barely any difference between there and the apartments."

"What you mean?"

"All summer long there are people walking up and down the streets, music blaring, fights. And didn't yo' daddy's car get broken into?"

"Yeah, but that was a minute ago. Can we at least look at it? Pleeease?" I could just imagine the LJ face he was making.

"I guess so. We can go by when I get off."

We did, and it was nice. But there was no way I was staying in that neighborhood.

That became a big issue between us. He wanted to stay on the north, and I wanted to get as far away from the north as possible. I just wanted to be able to pump my gas without someone trying to sell me something or five guys trying to holla at me and three out of the five cussing me out for telling them I have a man. I didn't feel safe over there anymore. The fact that he enjoyed it showed how different we really were. He went from calling me beautiful to calling me boujee. LaMar wasn't the only person to ever call me that, and I didn't look at it as an insult. It was just the way he said it.

When we went to look at the house I picked, he loved the house but hated the neighborhood.

"The house is cool, but I don't know about this, Toi," he said, rubbing his hand over his head.

"It was prefect! It's in a neighborhood with good schools and it actually has a two-car garage. You know I hate it when it hails. Plus no one can steal the car unless they break into the house. Not that we'd even have to worry about that."

"I know but it's so far away from our side. The north."

"Boy, it's on Council not in Tulsa. The north is just fifteen to twenty minutes away. It's practically down the street."

"I guess you've made up yo' mind."

"I really, really want it, baby."

"Okay, I guess."

A FEW MONTHS LATER, LAMAR AND I MOVED OUT OF OUR little two-bedroom apartment into a three-bed, one-and-a-half bath with a two-car garage rental home. It had an open concept, spacious living room, nice-sized kitchen, and a laundry room. No more toting our clothes to a laundromat. The bathroom in our room wasn't huge but had lots of storage space. We each had a closet, so my unorganized didn't have to mingle with his OCD. The boys had their own room. We had a fireplace and a nice backyard for the boys to play in. It felt amazing to me. Like I had accomplished something. I knew I could never go back to apartment life or the northside.

LaMar on the other hand still wasn't feeling it. "Man, I can't even bump my music over here."

"That's the point."

"It's so dull. Nobody is even outside. I went to the gas station and felt out of place."

"You'll get used to it. It's not like there aren't any black people out here."

"Yeah, but they're old black folks."

"No, they aren't. I saw the couple around the corner outside and they're our age. And the guy up the other way got a Cadi with rims on it. You're over exaggerating. I say give me dull and give me peace."

"That's not even how that quote goes."

"It is for me."

"I should've known yo' boujee ass would want to live somewhere like this."

"Hey, you can always go over to Malik's or yo' dad's and bump yo' music all yo' want. Just don't bring none of that stuff back here with you."

LaMar

Things with Toi and me hadn't been the greatest. When we first got together, we were so hot, heavy, and deeply in love. Then she started slacking. I knew she thought she was giving it up whenever I needed it, but sometimes I didn't even ask because of her bitchin'. I don't know if it was because of her job or the kids, but she seemed to have an attitude all the time. All I knew was I wasn't getting enough attention, and it was starting to make my eye wander. Every time I went over to Malik's, there were a few bad bitches over there all up in my face, and I had to say, "No, I got a woman." Sometimes I felt jealous of my big bro. He was free to be with anyone he wanted. I don't know what made me think I was ready for a committed relationship. Whatever spell Toi had put on me was starting to wear off.

Then we started trying to move and shit, and she really didn't respect my opinion. Yeah, she would ask me to look for spots but when I showed them to her it wasn't good enough. Always saying she didn't want to live in the neighborhood I wanted to live in. Which was stupid to me. So what a few cars got stolen or a couple of houses got broke into. That was my hood, and no one would disrespect me like that. They knew better after Malik and I checked the dude that broke into Pop's car.

When I saw the house she chose, it was what I pictured she would like. Boujee neighborhood of course. The house itself was nice but I felt uncomfortable and out of place. Way too straitlaced for my taste, but it was what she wanted. She couldn't have been happier when I agreed to it. I wanted her to feel comfortable and safe, but I wanted her to feel that way no matter where we lived as long as she was with me. It's like she didn't trust me or something.

Anyways, since she was paying the rent and the bills most the time, who am I to say no.

Still, it made me look at her differently. When I talked to my homie Chris and my brother Malik about it, they were no help.

"Yo' Mar, how you liking the new spot? I bet you're glad to be out the apartments," Chris said, rolling a blunt.

"Naw, man. My female got us way out on Council. There's barely any life out there. The house itself is straight though."

"You illin'. I wish I could find a female that elevates me. Shiiid, Toi got money, she's sexy, and she loves yo' dumb ass. I don't know why." Malik opened a beer as he flopped down onto the couch, almost spilling it.

"Whatever. You're just saying that because you wanted to hook up with her, and I beat yo' ass to it. She's a damn nag. She be wanting me to do too much."

"Like what?" Chris asked.

"Like work, help with the kids, cook, clean . . . you name it."

"This boy lyin'! When he's working, she don't even be sweatin' him. You just lookin' for a reason to be mad because she didn't want to move over this way."

"Man, whatever. You don't know what I go through. I love her and the kids, but I'm kinda tired of being a family man."

"Ain't nobody tell you to pump two babies into her." Malik laughed.

"The pussy too good to pull out or wear a condom," I said, and they laughed. "But for real, I'm thinkin' about movin' on. Relationships are too much work."

"Yo' ass just don't like working, whether that be on a job or a relationship," Chris explained and Malik laughed with him. "You're not going to find better than Toi." Chris sat back and lit the blunt.

I opened my mouth to cuss his ass out, but someone knocked on the door. Tracey, Kelly, and Melissa came walking they hot asses into the house, talkin' loud and racket. I was already dealing with enough shit, surely didn't want to see any of them. I looked behind Melissa and another female walked in and closed the door. She caught my eye immediately. She was cute, nice body, fat ass, little titties, short with pretty dark skin.

"Mia, that's Malik's brother, LaMar," Tracey said, waving in my direction.

Mia walked over and shook my hand, and I felt my dick stiffen a little. I noticed how full her lips were and started to imagine them wrapped around my dick.

"Nice to meet you." She smiled and sat down next to me.

The drinks started to flow, and the blunts were rolled and passed. I was impressed with how well Mia could hang. She was funny and comfortable around everyone, and I liked that. I turned on some Master P and the ladies started to dance. The thing that got me was when "Is There a Heaven for a Gangsta" came on, she knew every word. That shit was sexy as hell to me. Toi would never.

I got up and started to dance with her. She turned around and bent over in front of me, rubbing her ass all on my dick. I knew then she wanted me. I stepped outside for a minute, and it wasn't long before she came out.

"Why you out here?" she asked, sitting down on the step next to me, her top button unbuttoned more than it was when she arrived.

"Just chillin'. Gettin' kinda hot in there."

"So, what's up with you?"

"What you mean?"

"You fine or whatever. You single?"

She bold as fuck. "Naw."

"Damn. I hate to hear that. I was hoping to get to know you better." She reached over and ran her hand up my inner thigh, gently grazing my balls. She kept her hand there, and I didn't bother to move it.

I was a little shocked at how forward she was. I had just met her, and she was already pushing up on me hard. But fuck it. If she wanted to rub on my balls, it was cool with me.

"I mean, it's not all good at home." I leaned back and opened my legs wider to allow her more room to feel what she was trying to feel, happy I was wearing my basketball shorts.

"What's up then?" she asked, scooting closer to me. I could smell the cocoa butter on her skin. Her hand slid back and forth on my inner thigh. She knew what she was doing.

She lit a blunt, took a long drag, then passed it to me.

"Why aren't things good at home?" She put her hand back between my legs.

"Shiiidd, my girl be trippin' all the time. She doesn't respect me. And she be wanting me to do everything. Cook, clean, wash the cars, mow the grass. And every time I come over here to chill, she gets mad about that. I ask her to come, but she don't want to. She be actin' like I'm going to the strip club or something. I just be chillin'."

"That's crazy! Sounds like she's taking you for granted."

"That's what I'm sayin'. She don't appreciate nothing I do. Got me all stressed out and shit."

"That's sad."

It felt good for someone to take my side for a change.

The music was loud enough for us to hear outside and when Pretty Ricky's "On the Hotline" came on, she jumped up, stepped in front of me, and started dancing. She was throwing all that ass up in my face. I sat up to watch her. She was swayin' it side to side, droppin' it like it's hot. I have to admit, it was quite alluring. I reached out and rubbed her ass. It was soft. And when she didn't say anything, I smacked it and watched it jiggle. She turned her head, looked at me, and smiled. She pushed my legs closed, sat in my lap, and started bouncing her ass on me. I rubbed her thighs at first and then her ass some more. She leaned back and put my hand on her titty. I put the blunt down, and she put my other hand between her legs. I could already feel her heat and wetness through her biker shorts. I played with her clit a bit and she moaned.

"That feels good," she whispered and opened her legs wider.

She moved my hands, grabbed them, and stood up. "Come here."

I didn't want to stand up because my dick was rock hard at that point. When I did stand, her eyes went straight to my crotch. This time she gave me a sly smile and pulled me forward.

"Where we going?" I asked, allowing her to lead the way.

"I just want to talk to you in my car."

I jumped in the passenger side. She got in, turned on the car, and rolled the windows down but turned the music on low. I felt nervous sitting in the car with her the way she was looking at me. What if Toi rolled up?

"Promise" by Ciara came on, and I let her voice relax my mind. I knew Toi wasn't going to pop up. She didn't care enough to come over here to try and see what I was doing. Besides it was after eleven p.m.

"What you want to talk about that we couldn't talk about where we were at?" I asked, knowing damn well she didn't bring me to the car to talk. I hoped she didn't think I was going to give her the dick just because she gave me a little lap dance. I wasn't that easy. She reached over, trying to pull the string on my shorts.

"Hold up! What you doin'?" I grabbed her hand and looked at her like she was crazy.

"I just want to touch it," she said, licking her lips.

"Naw. I told you I got a girl."

"That's cool. I'm not going to tell yo' girl. Besides, it's not like I'm trying to sit on it. I just want to see what you workin' with. Let me see it." She started rubbing my dick. It got harder and was about to bust out my shorts.

"Girl, you on one. I just met you. I don't know you like that."

"I'm not going to try nothing crazy. I promise."

I let go of her hand and allowed her to continue to pull the string. I reached in and wrestled my dick out and laid it up on my stomach. I could see how impressed she was with my size.

"Damn, LaMar!" She started stroking me. "Did me dancing on you make him hard like this?"

Before I could answer, she leaned forward and wrapped her mouth around it. My eyes instantly rolled to the back of my head. I opened my mouth to tell her to stop, but all I could do was clear my throat. The warmth and wetness of her mouth made it hard to form words. *This is wrong. Why am I letting her do this? Toi would kill me if she found out.* But I couldn't stop. Truth be told, it felt good to have someone else do it. Not that Toi wasn't great at it, but it had been years since I had someone different.

I looked around to see if anyone was watching us as her head bobbing made my toes curl in my Jordans. People were out but she had parked towards the back under a tree, and it was dark. No one seemed to be looking in our direction. I looked down and watched her head pumping up and down. I relaxed enough to enjoy the sensations her efforts were sending through my body. She repositioned herself to get more of me into her mouth. Feeling the silkiness of it, I began to pump in and out of her face. I grabbed the back of her head and pushed it down so I could feel the suction in the back of her throat. I felt my ego boosted as she gagged on it.

"I'm about to cum," I whispered, but she didn't move. I pushed to the back of her throat one last time and felt myself release. "Fuck!" I said as I spilled into her mouth. She swallowed it down. That's something Toi had never done.

I let go of the back of her head and she slowly raised, wiping her mouth with her hand, averting her eyes from mine as if she was suddenly ashamed of what she had done.

I stuffed my dick back into my shorts. "I can't believe you just did that."

"Well, you said that you've been stressin'. I figured you could use a little stress relief. Besides, I didn't see you stoppin' me."

I felt guilty right away. Why the hell did I let things go so far? Didn't matter what had been going on with Toi and me. I loved her, and she didn't deserve this.

"You right. That was my bad. I gotta get going." I wasn't able to look at her either.

"I don't know why you are actin' like that. It's not like nobody saw us."

"I know, but still. I told you I got a girl."

"But she trippin' right? Anyways, I figured we could be friends. Or are you not allowed to have friends?"

"That didn't feel like you just wanting to be friends."

"I mean . . . I was thinkin' more like friends with benefits, but it's whatever."

"Oh, okay. That's what's up. We'll see." I opened the car door to get out.

"Put my number in your phone. Call me so we can hang out."

I took her number and got up out of there. I didn't even go back to Malik's apartment. I just left. On the way home, my heart was racing. I should have went in and took a shower or at least washed my dick before I left. I was slippin'. That was so fucked up of me. But that shit felt good as hell, and I needed it. I just had to make sure I stayed away from Toi when I got home.

Chapter 7

1999/00

While everyone else was worried about Y2K, I was worried about the turn things were taking in my relationship. LaMar was going out more. He lost his third job right after Thanksgiving for not going in on time. Again. Which pissed me off. He had to be there a couple hours after I left for work. So of course I'd wake him up before I'd leave, but he'd just go back to sleep.

I blamed myself. I'm the one who trained him to feel like it's no big deal if he lost his job. I got it. My bad, right? I was wrong for having my man's back. I felt as though I was being punished. After a while, a person gets tired of having to look the other way.

He started asking me for money as soon as I got home, so he could go "kick it." Hell, I came home tired and he was ready to leave. I understood he was home with the boys, but it wasn't like it was all day.

This is how his day went: got up at ten a.m., dressed, and fed the boys. Dropped LJ off at school by eleven a.m. and took Ty to daycare. Back home to play PlayStation NBA Live and smoke weed. No telling who all he had over with him. I came home early one day, and Malik and three other dudes were all up in the house playing, smoking, and eating up all the food I bought.

Anyways, he'd make dinner, go pick the boys up by four thirty, let them play for a little bit, and feed them so they were good until I got home.

I worked from nine to six, got home by around six thirty or seven. He might give me enough time to take a shower and eat. Not really in peace, because it was "Momma this" and "Momma that." After that, he was ready to go. Not saying it was every day. But it was heading that way.

The weekends were another story. It was mainly me and the boys all weekend with him being in and out. Sometimes he would stay out till two or three o'clock in the morning and because he called, he felt like that was okay. It wasn't. That caused us to fight more. The little time we did spend together, all he wanted to do was smoke. I didn't mind doing that every now and then. But every day, blunt after blunt? Nope. I kept wondering when he was going to grow up. Take care of his responsibilities. This was around the time I started telling everyone I had three kids. They would laugh when I told them the ages. Wasn't funny to me.

On New Year's Eve, LaMar talked me into going to a party that one of his friends was having. My mom kept the boys. I didn't like going to parties where there were a bunch of people I didn't know. However, he wanted me to go so I went. He knew everyone, which meant every chance he got he left me standing somewhere by myself.

"Babe, I'm going to go over here right quick and say hi to Chris," he'd say and off he'd go. Everyone was enjoying themselves doing the same shit he loved to do—drinking and smoking. I was paranoid, though I hadn't done anything but nurse one Crown and Coke. If somebody had called the police, we all would've gone to jail. You know that song "Here" by Alessia Cara? Hell, I could've written that song that night if I had the skills.

Once the damn ball dropped, I was so done. We kissed and I was ready to go. Of course, he got mad because he wanted to kick it all night. He went ahead and left with me. I'm sure he was thinking about going back the whole way home. I couldn't even wait for him to drive into the garage before opening the door to get out. I went in and got straight into the shower to wash my hair and get that smoke off me. I doubted I would ever be able to wear my little black dress again. When I came out and laid on the bed, he was standing there looking at me, eyes fire red, high, and half-ass drunk.

"I guess you ready to go to sleep, huh?"

"What else should I be ready to do, LaMar?" I'm sure he heard the tone in my voice.

"I mean, shiiiid." He grabbed himself. "The kids are gone for the night. Sooooo . . ."

I knew what he was getting at and honestly, I wasn't in the mood. But my momma always said, "If you don't take care of your man's needs, someone else will." My momma had these sayings that would pop into my head whenever the situation fit. So, I took care of him like I always did. I've *never* turned him down. Didn't matter if I was mad, tired, asleep, or in pain. If he wanted it, I did it. And that night was no different.

Afterward, while he was snoring, the thought of us not being together crossed my mind. I found myself thinking about that more and more every day. *I can do bad all by myself* was on repeat in my thoughts. I still loved him but even that feeling wasn't as strong as it used to be.

To check and see if I was overthinking, I explained things to the people closest to me—which I always told others to never do, but, hell, I was desperate.

"Why don't y'all gone and get married?" Momma asked me one day when I was complaining about how he was acting.

"Momma, I'm telling you I'm unhappy in my relationship and that's what you came up with? Why should I marry him?"

"Just to say you've been married."

What the hell would that fix? "Okay, Momma. LJ calling me. I'll call you back."

Why would I marry a man I wasn't even sure I still liked? Plus, he couldn't keep a job. I don't know what Momma was thinking when she said that. But I do know that's when I pretty much stopped listening to her. She had clearly lost her mind somewhere. I wanted a man I could depend on like LaMar could depend on me.

I called my Auntie Renee.

"Auntie, I just don't know what to do. I feel bad about not really feeling him like I used to. What advice do you have?"

"What yo' momma say?"

"Marry him."

"Huh? The hell wrong with her? They get *worse* after they put a ring on it. I need to call and check on yo' momma more often. She must be drinkin' in the daytime or something. But I don't know, baby. I've been telling you that you don't need no regular working man no way. I can hook you up with one of Jabir's rich friends and we could travel the world together."

"What about my kids?"

"They can come too."

"Auntie, I don't know. I've never been with anyone outside our race. I don't even know if I would feel comfortable with that."

"Chile, the amount of money they have can make you comfortable. Trust me. Reeeal comfortable."

"Wouldn't that make me a hoe though?"

"No. Hoes have sex with strangers for money. You would be having sex with yo' husband for money. That's completely different."

As y'all can see, she was no help.

I spoke to Kēssa about it. We were still cool, although we didn't kick it like we used to. Single motherhood took up all her time. She's one of the reasons I stayed with LaMar.

Every time I talked to her it was, "Girl, you don't want this life. You know their sorry-ass daddy is never around. I know you think because you make good money, you don't need him, but trust me, it's more to it than that. Imagine having to work your full-time job, cook, clean, pick them up and drop them off . . . all that. He's good for something."

Which was true. There's a lot I didn't have to do because of him. And that should be enough, right? But for some reason, it wasn't. It had never bothered me before. Why was it bothering me so bad now?

Chapter 8

Introducing Dena

Ricky had become a welcomed friend. He made sure to come by my office as often as he could, and we'd talk. We'd have lunch together. Nothing serious, just friends. It was nice having a male I could confide in and get advice from. And him flirting with me didn't hurt my feelings either. Things at home with LaMar weren't fun anymore. We were barely even touching. The last time I caught him staring at me, he had an annoyed look on his face. No longer the sweet look of love.

I don't know if y'all remember Cadena. She's the lady I admired who announced my promotion. Well, after that we didn't talk or collaborate much. She'd email if she had a question on a report I did, or if she needed more info on something. When we were in managers' meetings, and she stood up to speak, she'd still talk about how much she loved her job. I could hear the joy in her tone. All I could think about was how Dwayne and I used to talk about her.

Dwayne would say, "They must be paying her a whole lot more money than they pay us. Why she feel she needs to be so damn happy every time she talks to us?"

"I know, right? Maybe she's sleeping with her boss and it's

good as hell!" I'd say, and we'd both laughed. I kinda missed those days. But I didn't miss that paycheck.

Anyways, we became the best of friends. The way it happened was kinda funny.

Y'all know I saw her as that one black person in the company who talked and acted like she wasn't raised around very many other black people. To put it into perspective, have you ever heard Lil Jon when he talks? Yeah, it's like that. Like "pass the Grey Poupon" proper.

I was wrapping things up for the day when Ricky came to me.

"Hey, I'm going to Cadena's house after work to kick it. I want you to come with me."

I just stared at him with a blank face. I was positive she and I would have nothing in common. She probably sat around listening to opera music while having conversations about politics and sipping on sherry like Frasier and his brother do on the show.

"Why would I want to go over to Cadena's?" I asked, blinking rapidly.

"She cool people." He laughed at my reaction.

"I don't know if she's my kind of people. Then again, I don't know her." After a few minutes of us staring at each other in silence, I said, "Yeah, why not. I'm not doing anything after work."

I didn't have a life outside of kids and LaMar. I didn't really hang out with Kēssa but once every blue moon, and I really didn't have any other friends, so I agreed.

I hit up LaMar and let him know I wouldn't be coming straight home.

"Where you going?" He sounded frustrated. I'm sure he was waiting for me to come home so he could leave.

"One of the women here invited me out for drinks. I told you about Cadena," I lied.

"The black white lady? You going to have drinks with her?"

"First of all, she's not white, she just speaks extremely proper and speaking proper doesn't change yo' race. And yeah. Why not?"

"Man, I was trying to go over to Malik's and watch the game."

"Damn! Can I do something other than work and come home for once? You always going over to Malik's for something. I need some me time too."

"I guess. Don't come home different. You boujee enough as it is."

"Boy, bye." I hung up and waved Ricky in.

"You ready?"

"As I'm going to get."

"You might want to close yo' shades." He nodded toward the window, looking out at Craven's office. "Dude nosey. He looking all up in here."

"Boy, that man ain't looking in this direction. His desk is just facing this way." I wished he would look at me. "I keep that open so I can look at him."

"You *my* work wife. Don't let me catch yo' eyes wandering." He closed the blinds for me.

I followed him over to Cadena's. It wasn't in the kind of neighborhood I thought she'd be living in. I figured she'd be in a big house in a gated community.

We both stepped out of the car. He took my hand and walked me to the door. I remember thinking his hand was soft and warm. We stepped up onto the porch and I heard "Killing Me Softly" by the Fugees playing loudly from inside.

"Are we at the right house?"

"Yeah. Why you ask me that?" I knew he knew why I was asking.

"Just wondering."

He didn't raise his hand to knock but instead grabbed the doorknob.

"Wait. You just gone walk in?"

"Yelp. I got it like that." He smiled and swung the door open. Someone was in the back singing the song loudly, off tune but with feeling. Ricky picked up the remote off the table and turned the music down.

"Who's there?"

"It's me! Were you waiting for someday else?"

"Yeah! Jesus with the man I prayed for last night! I'm in the den!" she shouted back.

I whispered, "Who's that? Her sister?"

"Naw, that's her."

He pulled me toward the back of the house. When we walked through the doorway, Cadena was sitting on the couch, makeup off, still wearing her wig of the day with sweats and a T-shirt on. She looked pretty much the same except for two things: she didn't look like her professional, well-put-together self. Which was cool because she was at home chillin'. But the other thing was she was licking a blunt closed.

She smoke? And what happened to her voice? I don't know what I was expecting. I guess I pictured her walking towards us in a long silk robe, holding a glass of wine, sounding like Mrs. Doubtfire when she said hello.

"I brought a friend," Ricky announced.

She looked up and smiled. "Hey, Toi!" She put the blunt on the table, stood up, and gave me a hug. "Ricky told me he might bring you. Have a seat."

I sat down, feeling a little stunned. I never would've guessed work was all a facade. She did it so well.

She picked the blunt back up and sat back. "You smoke?"

"A little."

She fired it up. "Ricky, don't just sit there. Go make us some drinks."

Ricky stood and asked, "You straight?"

"Boy, gone. You act like I'm going to do something to her. Toi knows me," she said, muggin' him and waving him out the room. "So, Toi, it's good to see you outside of work. How are you liking being a boss?"

"I love it!"

"Girl, me too!" she said, blowing out smoke.

"I used to think you were crazy when you talked about how much you loved your job. But I get it now."

"I'm not surprised. No one gets it till they're in the position."

She handed me the blunt. I could tell by the smell it was strong, so I took a small puff and still almost coughed up a lung. I quickly handed it back to her.

"That's that good," she said, laughing.

I was just happy Ricky came back with my drink. "Okay, I have to ask . . . why you sound so different at work?"

"Girl, that's my work voice. You don't have one?"

"Naw."

"I used to really talk like that. I had to learn how to be regular. You ever meet my momma you'll understand why."

We sat back and really talked. We found out we had a lot in common. For example, her husband Keyon and LaMar came from the same hometown of Hugo. He was taking her through as much shit as LaMar was taking me through. Keyon could keep a job, but he couldn't keep his dick in his pants. That's why she had filed for divorce. But for some reason, they were still living together.

Neither of us could figure out why we were staying. She was the only one who seemed to understand what I was going through, and we became really close from then on. Ricky still reminds us that it was him who brought us together, like we owe him something.

Chapter 9

I'm Done

LaMar

Y'all, I fucked around and called Mia and had been kicking it with her for a few months. She was cool, and we had fun together. She smoked as much as, if not more than, I did. She could out-drink most dudes but not be sloppy, and hood shit didn't bother her since she was from the hood. It was nice to kick it with her. We had a lot in common. Toi had an outgoing personality too, but Mia's was just different.

I found myself lying to Toi more and more. Hell, I stayed out till three or four a.m. most nights. Of course, that made me and Toi fight more. I just couldn't help it. I felt trapped at home.

I wasn't with Mia every night, but even when I was trying to simply chill with my homies, she always seemed to find me. I would be parking lot pimpin' outside of the club—you know sittin' out in the parking lot hollering at females—and she'd pull up out of nowhere. Or I'd be chillin' over at Chris's and here came Mia and her friends. She'd come in and stay stuck under me as much as possible. Especially if there was any other females around. She acted like she was marking her territory. The shit had to stop.

I messed up and had sex with her a couple of times. Both times I was drunk. I really wasn't even feelin' her like that. I just did it so she'd stop begging for it. It wasn't as good as it was with Toi. Her mouth wet but the pussy was a little dry. Probably from all that weed she'd be smokin'.

I was getting tired of her all up in my face. One night outside the club, she pulled one of her popups while I was sitting in the car with one of my homegirls, and she acted a fool. She was trying to fight the girl and everythang. I knew then that she wanted it to be more than I was willing to give. After that, I avoided her. I didn't answer her calls or texts. I wasn't hangin' with Chris or Malik so she couldn't find me. If I went anywhere, it was over to Pop's house. I wanted some time alone to figure out what I was doing. I damn sure didn't want to see Mia. Pops didn't allow us to smoke in his house, so I went out to the car to smoke. One day I was laid back in my car, eyes closed, at peace, smokin'. Mystical comes on the radio hollerin' "Danger," when she knocked on my window.

"Mar!"

I jumped up and stared at her. *How the fuck did she find me?*

"What's up?"

"Open the door. I need to talk to you."

"I really don't feel like talkin'."

"Please, Mar."

I popped the locks, and she hopped in. I laid my head back and closed my eyes.

"I've been trying to call and text you for over a week now. Why haven't you answered me back?"

"Because you've been on one lately."

"What you mean?"

"Poppin' up everywhere I go. I mean, look at what you just did. How you find me anyway? I've never brought you over here."

"I was on my way over to my friend's house and saw your car. I just got out to see if you were in here."

"Why though? I haven't been responding. That didn't tell you nothing?"

"No. How am I supposed to know what's going on if you don't say nothin'?"

"You already know. What happened the last time I saw you?"

"I know I was tweakin' and drunk. I saw that girl in your car and got all in my feelings. I've been trying to apologize for that, but you won't—"

"That shit was unacceptable! I'm not yo' man!"

"I know but—"

"But you acting like I am. All up on me in public. All it would take is for one of Toi's friends to see that shit, and I won't get to see my kids no more. I'm not gone keep risking shit with you."

"I'm sorry. I said I was drunk."

"It wasn't just that, Mi. It's everything. You texting me all hours of the night. You know I'm at home. Again, poppin' up everywhere I go. I already got one female trippin'. I don't need or want another one. We're supposed to be friends, remember?"

"You right. I shouldn't have been doing all that."

"You damn right. That's why we gotta chill."

"What you mean by 'we gotta chill'? You don't want to kick it no mo'?"

"Nope."

"Oh, so you get what you want and that's it?"

I looked over at her. "Get what I want? I really didn't want it if I'm being honest. I did that for you."

"I can't believe you just said that!" She started tearing up. "I thought we were better than that! You weren't saying that when I was riding you!"

"Wait . . . I'm sorry. Don't cry. That didn't come out right." I just wanted to calm her. I didn't need her making a scene. "Look, I'm just stressing. But I do mean it when I say we don't need to see each other anymore. Like I said, I got too much shit to deal with already. You seem like you trying to find a man, and I'm not that."

"I thought you were really feelin' me, but I guess not."

"You cool, Mia. I'm just not trying to do what you are. I'm not leaving my family."

"Leavin' yo' fam? Oh, but you not with her like that, right?"

"What that got to do with my boys? See, I knew you didn't really feel me when I was talkin' to you."

"I was—"

I put up my hand to stop her from talkin'. "It's all good. But I'm done."

"You know what? Fuck you, LaMar! I got plenty of dudes who want this!" She jumped out of my car and slammed the door.

The relief I felt when she got out was unmeasurable. I was tired of her acting like we were something we weren't. I made up my mind right then that I was going to chill. I wasn't going to be kicking it as much. I was going to try to get things back right between Toi and me. Go back to showing her the love she might've forgotten I had for her. I was never trying to have an affair with Mia. Just needed some different energy.

Chapter 10

Intuition

Things weren't getting any better with LaMar. I think he wanted the summer off so he could hang out with his homeboys. He was kicking it more and more. Staying out later and later. We were fighting constantly because he claimed he was trying to get a job, but I couldn't tell. I came home early one day, and he was gone. When he did show up, I asked where he'd been, and he claimed that he was out filling out applications. He had on a T-shirt and some shorts. I called bullshit.

He was acting different too. He wasn't catering to me at all anymore. We basically stopped having sex. It went from a few times a week to barely once a week. I didn't want to go out because I was always paying for it. He didn't even ask me to come watch him play ball at the gym anymore. We were like two ships passing. I would come in and he would head out.

One night while he was out, he butt dialed me. His phone was obviously in his pocket because I heard voices but couldn't understand what was being said. Have you ever received a butt call and sat there and listened until it hung up? I did. I listened for thirty minutes. I heard him talking and laughing, I think I heard Malik's ass, and I know I heard some females. Then he picked up his phone and said, "Oh shit," and hung it up. I tried calling back several times, but he didn't answer, which was also becoming his norm. So, I waited up for his ass.

Around three in the morning he came creeping in the house trying to be all quiet and shit. I was sitting on the couch in the dark.

"Did you have fun?"

"Fuck, Toi! You scared the shit out of me! What you doin' still up?" He closed and locked the door.

"What you doin' still out?"

"What you mean? I was kickin' it with Malik."

"And?"

"And that's it." He hurried to our bedroom.

I hurried right behind him. "You a damn lie. You butt dialed me. I heard bitches in the background."

"That was probably music. There was a whole bunch of people outside, so it could have been next door. You know how it is over there."

"Why did you say 'Oh shit' before you hung up yo' phone then?" I asked, jumping up on the bed as he took his clothes off.

"I don't even know what you talkin' about."

"Mm-hmm. So why didn't you answer when I called? It could have been an emergency."

"I didn't hear it."

"Keep lyin' to yo'self. I know you were with some bitch!"

"Man, don't start that shit! Ain't nobody doing nothing with no bitches!"

"Whatever, LaMar! Don't get caught slippin'!" I turned over in the bed.

"You stayed up just to tell me that? Hello?"

I ignored him. I was too angry to talk at that point. Ain't no damn way he didn't hear that phone. That was the lie he always told. That shit had been happening way too often, and I was getting tired of it.

He went into the bathroom and by the time he came out, I

pretended to be asleep. But I didn't sleep at all that night. My gut was telling me he had been cheating on me.

~

A COUPLE OF WEEKS LATER, I WAS ON MY WAY TO Dena's when he passed me. I know I saw a female in the car. I almost broke my neck trying to see who it was. I hurried and made a U-turn, but I lost him. I got to Dena's and told her what happened.

"See? Woman's intuition ain't no joke. If you feel like he's cheating, he's cheating."

My head was pounding. "I don't want to believe things have gotten that bad, sis. Why would he do me like that? I do everything for him."

"Because he has a dick and that's what the dick tells them to do. I swear that's where the brain is located. Either that or when it gets hard it drains the blood strictly from the part of the brain that gives them common sense. Either way, they stupid. Call him and see what he say."

I was nervous and kinda hoping he wouldn't answer. But for once he did. "I'm surprised you answered the phone."

"You threatened to disconnect it if I don't start answering, remember?"

"As she should!" Dena yelled.

"Ah hell, you with D?"

"Never mind that. Where you at?"

"Malik's."

"Liar, liar pants on fire!" Dena chanted.

"D, hush please!" I said.

"He lyin' though." She lit up a blunt.

"I saw you over on Hefner, and you weren't going in the direction of Malik's. Who was that in the car with you?"

"Huh?"

"Boy, if you can 'huh' you can hear! Who was the bitch in the car?" Dena asked, grabbing the phone.

"Wasn't no bitch in my car!"

"See, you lyin'! She saw you about fifteen minutes ago! Who was it, LaMar? Huh?"

"Man, can I talk to Toi, please?"

I snatched the phone back. "Well?"

"That was . . . ummm . . . Felicia. You know Felicia. The one that stay next door to Malik. I was just running her to the store."

Dena snatched the phone back. "Why didn't you just say that in the first place?"

"I wasn't thinking about it."

"Yo' ass still lyin'!"

I took the phone back. "So that was just Felicia?"

"Yeah. We just went up to the sto' to get some blunt sticks and beer. That's it."

I have to admit, I felt a sense of relief. But deep inside I knew he was lying.

When I got off the phone with him, Dena was heated. "You fell for the banana in the tailpipe bullshit, didn't you?"

"I didn't see who it was, D."

"I remember when I was naïve like you. Wasn't cute on me either."

A month went by, and it was more of the same—him in and out, coming home all hours of the night. Then it just suddenly stopped. I looked up and he was coming home at nine, ten o'clock. Some nights he didn't go nowhere at all. He was cooking and actually sticking around to have dinner. He was going to Blockbuster and renting movies, rubbing my feet after work, asking me about my day, playing with the kids and putting them to bed, giving me time to myself. He went back to calling me beautiful instead of boujee. It was almost like he did a full 360°. I was eating it up too. We were back to having sex again and not just regular sex—it was sex with foreplay. And for the first time in what seemed like forever, he was saying that he loved me again.

Oh course, Dena wasn't feeling it.

"He up to something. He probably got a baby on the way."

"Dena, don't say shit like that."

A FEW WEEKS OF HAVING MY MAN BACK DID ME SOME good. I was sitting in my office, finally having a moment to myself, when Dena came busting in, out of breath.

"Girl, are you busy?"

"No, just working. Is somebody chasing you? And if so, why you lead them to my office?" I said, smiling.

"No, but if they were I would lead them here so they could get both of us and take us out our misery. But for real, this is important." She closed the door and leaned forward on the back of one of the chairs in front of my desk. "Has LaMar taken you to get some of that spring water from Hugo? The water that comes out the ground ice cold?"

"Out by the lake? Yeah. We got a few jugs the last time we went out there to visit his mom's people. It's good fresh water."

"Girl, stop drinking that damn water! I figured it out! That's how they get us to stay with them!"

"You're telling me that the spring water is used to brainwash us into staying with them?"

"Hell, yeah!! Think about it. I don't know about you, but whenever I get mad at Keyon and I'm at the point where I want to smash his damn face in, the bastard brings me a cup of that damn water! The next thing I know, we chillin' and laughin' like nothing ever happened."

"You sure that's not part of that split personality you have?"

She ignored my comment. "How about every time we go down there, we gotta bring home jugs of that shit! Something ain't right about it!"

She did have a point. The last time we went down there, LaMar went out to the spring and pumped six jugs of water. We got on the road to head back home and about twenty minutes into the ride he says, "Fuck! I gotta turn around!"

"For what?" I asked.

"I forgot the damn water!" He looked around for a place to get off the highway and turn around.

"So? We can buy water. We'll get some next time. I don't see why we have to go back for that."

"I sat there and pumped all those jugs. I'm going back to get it."

And he did too. Even though I was laughing at Dena's presentation, it was one of those things that makes you go, *hmmmm*.

"You laughin', I'm like *super* serious! Don't say I didn't tell you. You have been warned." She did a little spin and walked out the door.

A few minutes later my desk phone rang. I figured she had something else to say about the water.

"This is Toi."

"Toi?" asked a female voice I'd never heard before.

"Yes?"

"Look, don't get mad, please." I knew then it was about to be some shit. "My name is Mia and I know LaMar. Actually, me and LaMar have been seeing each other for about three months. He tells me that y'all live together, but you not together. I'm tired of feeling like he's lying to me."

My heart dropped into my stomach. I was hoping I didn't have to worry about that and now some bitch was calling me at work. Really?

"Mia, right? Well, Mia, if that's what he's telling you, he's a damn lie. We're together."

"I knew it! He claims he be sleeping on the couch. He's there because he wants to be in his kids' life and if he left, you wouldn't let him see them."

"And you believed that?"

"Yeah. He be over here late, ignoring your calls, telling me how you're always trippin' and how you don't appreciate him. So why wouldn't I believe it? We're together all the time." Soon as she said "trippin'" I knew he said it.

"Ain't no damn way I would believe a man is living with his baby's mother, going home to her every night—no matter how late—but they not fuckin'."

"He said he wants to be with me and he's tired of being around you. Since it was taking him so long to tell you, I figured I should call and talk to you myself. I really care about him and from what he says you don't so . . ."

"It's taking everything in me not to call you outa yo' name right now. You believed that sorry excuse because you wanted to. I will say this, I don't know how you got my number, but I don't appreciate you calling me with this shit at my job. Now, I do appreciate you letting me know what's up, and I'm gone handle him. You can have his sorry ass! Hope you're ready to take care of him because he don't work. But either way, don't call my job again!"

I was so discombobulated I couldn't even remember what the hell I was doing before the hoe called me. I started to call his ass and hung up. I needed to talk to him face to face, so I gathered my things and headed out early.

Chapter 11

It's On Now

When I hit the corner, I saw his car in the driveway. I swooped up in there so fast, I almost hit the garage door. I knew then that I needed to sit back and chill for a minute. This was the second time some bitch had approached me about him fucking with them, plus the one time I saw him with a bitch, and I'm not going to keep going through this shit.

The first time I was approached by another woman about LaMar, I was at the grocery store with my kids. I kept feeling like someone was watching me. I'd look around and see them duck behind something or hurry and move past the aisle I was on. Finally, she came and acted as if she was looking for something on the shelf behind me.

"Yo' name Toi, huh?" she asked, popping her gum.

I turned and looked at her. She was kinda short with fire-red hair. She didn't even try to make it look natural. She had on some extra-short shorts and a dirty-ass tank top. She looked stanky and ratchet.

"Who's asking?"

"Oh, I'm Sheeta. I'm a friend of your boyfriend, LaMar."

"A friend, huh? And how do you know him?"

"We met at his friend's house a few weeks back."

"Okay . . ."

"So, you are his baby momma, but are you his girlfriend?"

"Didn't you just say you're friends with *my* boyfriend? Did I correct you?" I said with a tone.

"Hey, you don't have to get no attitude with me! I'm just asking since he's been trying to hook up with me!"

"Oh, really?"

"Yeah, he called me late the other night asking if he could come chill. It was twelve o'clock at night. Ain't but one thang to do that late. But I don't do drama, so I told him no." The bitch was poppin' that gum and my nerves. I silently wished she'd bite her damn tongue. But I could tell she was a pro at it.

"That's what's up! I appreciate you letting me know."

She walked off giggling and shit, which made me wonder if there was more to it than she was telling me.

I went straight home. He came to help get the groceries out the car, smiling at me, oblivious. I was heated but had to wait for the right time to bring it up. I didn't want to wake the boys, who had fallen asleep on the way home.

We put them in their beds and went into the kitchen to put the food away. As I unloaded the bag of canned goods, I picked up a can of corn and thought to throw it at him, but I didn't. Instead, I said, "Some chick named Sheeta approached me in the store."

"Sheeta?" he asked, playing stupid. I saw him cut his eyes over at me when he heard her name.

"Yeah, she said she met you at somebody's house and you were trying to hook up with her." I calmly put it out there like I wasn't mad, but I was.

He didn't even flinch. "Oooh, Sheeta! She short, kinda hood-lookin' with fire-red hair?"

"Yeah, that's her."

"Man, whatever! That girl crazy! She's been pushing up on

me for a minute now! I didn't try to do nothing with her! I already told that girl I got a wifey at home!"

"Let me find out you fucking around!"

"Ain't nobody fucking around on you! Did she say we were fuckin'?"

"No, she said you were trying to. So why she go all out her way to come tell me that?"

"Because she's a messy-ass chicken-head who mad that I won't give her none!" He stopped and looked at me. "You believe that shit, huh? You really sittin' up in here mad!" He came over to me and wrapped his arms around my waist. "Baby, why the hell would I try and get with someone like that when I got all this good woman right here? You know how much our family means to me." He started kissing me on my neck and playing with my nipples, which is my spot. "I don't need nobody messing up what I got." He turned me around and kissed me, took me by the hand into the bedroom, locked the door, and bent me over the bed. That pretty much shut me up about it.

Now here we were a few months later, and I'm wondering if that was Mia in the car with him or a third hoe.

I tried hard to get my thoughts together. My mind was racing. I was not gone cry as Mary J said. I got out of the car slowly to steady myself. I felt nauseous. How could he do that to me with everything I did for his sorry ass? I knew something wasn't right.

When I walked in, he was sitting on the couch playing a damn video game. He paused it and looked over at me. He dropped the controller and hurried toward me when he saw the look on my face.

"What's wrong, baby?" He tried to touch me, but I flinched and pushed his hands away.

I took a deep breath. "I got a call at work from Mia." The look on his face changed. I could tell he was thinking hard and fast.

"Who?"

"You heard me! The girl you've been fucking for a few months now!" She hadn't told me that, I just assumed.

"Man, you trippin'! I don't know what you're talking about." He wouldn't even look at me, so I knew he was lying.

"Don't try to turn this around on me like I'm crazy!" Silence. "So, you don't have nothing to say! Some hoe calls me at work telling me you're fucking her and all you got is I'm trippin'?" He stood there looking dumb. "Well?"

"Maaan . . This is some bullshit!"

"You have been fucking her, haven't you? I can't believe this shit!"

"You was slippin' so I . . ." He said it under his breath, shrugging his shoulders.

"Excuse me?"

"Okay, baby look . . ." He looked down at the floor. "I kicked it with her, but we didn't do nothing!"

"You're a damn lie! She told me you said we weren't together, and you were only here for the kids. Oh, and you sleeping on the couch? For real? You not fuckin' her but you're at her house all hours of the night ignoring my calls. That part is true, right? She lying about y'all fuckin' though, huh? And I'm the dumbest bitch you know. You man enough to do it, but you not man enough to admit it?" I said, kickin' at his ego.

"Man, like I said we just kicked it a few times."

His lies were making me madder. I had to hear him admit it.

"She told me where the mole is on your inner thigh! I already know the truth. I want to hear you tell me what's up. You don't want to be with me no more, then you can leave!" If he could lie, so could I.

"Okay, baby, I fucked up! I've messed around with her, but I don't give a damn about her! I love you!" He had the nerve to drop to his knees.

You really do have to be careful what you wish for because him saying that was like a gut punch to my soul. I had to walk away and sit down. I looked around for somewhere to go that was away from him. The hurt was turning into rage. I literally saw red. Being a Taurus, that couldn't be a good sign.

I went toward the bedroom.

"Toi? Toi! Are you going to let me explain?"

He hopped up off the floor to come after me and got to me just as I was closing the door. We both pushed on it—I was trying to close it so I could lock him out, and he was trying to keep me from closing it. I got tired of the back and forth, so I gave up and let it go. I walked over to the bed and sat down, looking at the floor, trying to hold back my tears. They weren't tears of pain, at least not all of them. I don't know why when I get mad, I cry. Again, he kneeled in front of me, trying to grab my hands.

"Don't touch me, LaMar!"

"Baby, I'm so, so sorry! I thought you were losing love for me. We're always fighting about me not working or not trying hard enough. I felt like less of a man. She looked at me like you used to. To her, I wasn't some sorry-ass nigga living off her. That's what was going through my head. I needed to feel something different." He got in my face. "Baby, please look at me, please."

I didn't know if I'd ever be able to look at him again without putting my hands on him. I heard Momma's voice say, *Don't put yourself in a man's place unless you're ready to be treated like one.* Hell, I felt ready.

"I think you should get your shit and go live with her. See how long that look of you being the man stays in her eyes. I wasn't losing love for you because you weren't working. I was losing respect because you weren't trying."

"That's what I'm saying, though! I could feel that! I was hurt!"

"So, this is your way of getting back at me for being disappointed in you? You could've left if that was the case. But this?"

"I wasn't trying to get back at you. I was trying to fix something in me."

"All you had to do was get a job, not a side hoe! You stickin' yo' dick in another bitch made you feel more like a man? Not taking responsibility and stepping up to take care of your family?

Boy, get out my face with that shit!" I pushed his face as hard as I could.

He grabbed my hands. "You're right! I was wrong for that. What can I do to fix this? I'll do whatever you ask. But please, don't make me leave my fam. I'm not trying to be with her! It's not like that. I had already told her it was over. Look! Hold on . . ."

He stood, picked up his Nokia, and called her.

"Mia? What the hell? You called my wife at her job!" he yelled as soon as she answered.

"Yeah. So what? You said y'all weren't together anymore! I was tired of you lying, so I asked her!" I heard her yell back.

"Okay, you right, I lied! I am still with her, so don't worry about seeing or talking to me ever again!"

"Whatever! Don't act like I did something wrong with your triflin' ass! I knew you wasn't shit! She had a right to know and so did I! So fuck you!"

He calmed his voice. "You right. Why am I even screaming at you? I did this. I am the one who is in the wrong here. I can't even be mad at you. You did what you felt you had to do. But I told you a minute ago it was over. I haven't even talked to you in a couple of months. So I don't know why you even did that."

"You didn't even really give a good reason. Everything you said I could've changed! But it was just over and that was it! After all them times I held yo' ass while you cryin' about how she always trippin', how she don't believe in you no mo'! You got me fucked up callin' me wildin' out!"

"Like I said, I was wrong for ever kickin' it with you. And don't be making it sound like we were together all the time. I don't know what you thought was going to happen when you called her. What? You thought I was going to leave my family to be with you? You must be crazy! I'm not going to keep going back and forth with you about this shit. It's done!"

"LaMar, wait—" she said as he was hanging up in her face. She tried to call back a few times but eventually gave up.

"See, baby? She only called you because I told her I didn't want to talk to her anymore. I couldn't keep doing you like that. You didn't deserve it, and I didn't want to lose you."

Him saying that brought back everything I had been through with Samir. Another déjà vu moment.

"Oh, so that's supposed to make me feel better about you fuckin' some other bitch? News flash . . . it don't! You need to go!"

"Go where?"

"Gone and be with her! I don't give a fuck where you go at this point! You need to get out of here!"

"Oh, so it's over? It's like that?"

"Yelp!"

"Naw, baby! Don't be like that! You and the boys mean the world to me! And I swear on my life, nothing like this will ever happen again! Please give me another chance. Please!" He dropped to his knees in front of me again. "I'm never going to talk to her again, I swear!"

"She still got your number."

"I'll call and get my number changed!"

"You still know where she lives. The bitch better not know where we live!"

"Baby, damn! I'm not that dirty! I wouldn't bring some random to our house!"

"How would I know that? Apparently, I don't even know you! I've been getting played for months and didn't know it! I can't believe you did this! All the shit I do for you, and this is what you do? I buy you food, clothes, help you with gas, give you money for your weed! I pay every time we go out! I open my legs whenever you ask no matter how I feel! I treat yo' ass like a king even though you can't do the same for me and you fuck around on me? Guess I've been paying for you to go fuck her too, huh?" Saying that out loud made me madder. I wanted to reach out and pull the skin off his face. He needed to get away from me.

"Why you gotta go there? I appreciate everything you do,

baby! I put it on my life—hell, I put it on my dick, I will never see that bitch again! I told you I been done stopped a long time ago!" He started crying again. Fake-ass tears.

"You can put it on whatever you'd like, but you still gotsta go. You have no idea what level of heated I am right now. So, what I'm gone do is take a shower. I want your ass gone when I come out." I spoke calmly.

"Oh, so I don't get another chance?" He wiped his tears and moved out the way to keep me from stepping on him.

That stopped me in my tracks. I turned and looked through him and asked, "If I would've done the same to you, what would you do?" He simply hung his head. "Exactly!"

I went into the bathroom and locked the door. I turned on the shower and undressed. I could still hear him in the room moving around. I stepped in and thought about all the times he came home late, all the times I called and he didn't answer, the money I gave him to go kick it—was he with her every time? I could no longer hold back the tears. I stood there and cried.

I was sad but relieved to see he was gone when I came out of the bathroom.

Chapter 12

He Tried It

LaMar got some of his stuff and went to Malik's. He was still picking up the boys at daycare. I would stop by on my way home from work to get them. A few nights a week he would keep them with him. That gave me time to think about whether or not I wanted to even try to forgive him. Truth be told, I missed him like crazy but hated the sight of him at the same time. When I would pick up the kids, he would try to talk to me, but I still couldn't look at him. Much less hear what he had to say.

I was so hurt, I didn't want to do anything but go to work and go home. I found myself hiding away from everyone and spending most of my nights crying alone in my bed. I couldn't eat, I barely slept, and I avoided my friends and family. It took a week before I could even tell anyone what happened. I called Kēssa first since she'd been there from day one.

"Girl, men fuck up all the time. That's what they do. But he's begging for your forgiveness. You know he called me crying, asking me to talk to you for him? That boy loves you so much! That's all he kept saying. How much he loves you and the boys. Hell, I wish somebody loved me like that. He wasn't even messing with her for that long."

"That's because she busted him out! It's not like he confessed. He'd still be messing with her if she wouldn't have called me."

"No, he wouldn't have. He told me the whole story. He had been stopped messing with her. She was just mad and wanted to mess y'all up."

"Well, it worked. I don't care if he hadn't messed with her in a year. He shouldn't've done it at all. I've never done him like that."

"What about LJ and Ty? They love they daddy."

"They used to him being gone, so they'll be alright."

"Still, you should at least talk to him."

When I told Dena, she came right over. I was sitting in the living room crying my eyes out, listening to "All Cried Out" by Lisa Lisa and Cult Jam and singing the hell out that song. I didn't even hear her come in.

Right in the middle of singing my heart out, the song went off. I turned, and she was standing there shaking her head. I flopped down on the couch. "Turn it back on. It was getting to the good part."

"I got a song you can sing. 'Can you . . . feel a . . . brand new daaay!'" She flailed her arms and skipped around the room a few times. Like she was straight out of the movie *The Wiz*. She flopped down next to me on the couch, out of breath, and fired up a blunt. "Where you even find that old-ass song? Here, smoke this."

I took the blunt and inhaled, but the tears kept falling.

"I don't understand why you're so upset. I'm glad he's gone! I was so sick and tired of him using you. I was about to cut his brake line but then I had to remember y'all got kids."

"I don't understand why it's okay in his mind to do me of all people like that though. What I do that was so wrong?" I asked crying.

"I know you not blaming yourself for his fuck-up."

"I just wonder what it was about her. Was she prettier than me? I mean what was it? I know she wasn't taking care of him like I was."

"Girl, none of that makes any difference. He told you it was all on him and it was. One of the times Keyon cheated on me, I thought everything was perfect. We weren't fighting, we were having sex every other day—sometimes twice. We were going out and having fun together. We were traveling. Hell, when I found out, I couldn't figure out how he found the time or the energy. I knew I didn't do nothing wrong, and the chick wasn't all that. It's just new pussy. She was the opposite of me."

"I still don't understand why."

"Some things are not for us to understand, sis. God showed you who he is. Believe it. Some people are in your life for a blessing, some for a lesson. He just so happened to be the latter. LJ and Ty were your blessings. That's what he was here to do." She blew smoke in my face and wiped my tears.

"I really love him, D," I said, now ugly crying. Hard.

She pulled me in. "Woo woo woo." She patted my back, sounding like Synclaire from *Living Single*. "It's okay to love his punk ass from a distance. As soon as you get the rest of that spring water out yo' system, you are going to be just fine. Listen to me. You're a beautiful woman, you have a bangin' body, yous smart, funny, and too good for his ass."

"I don't want to have to start over. And what about the boys?"

"Stop acting like you don't have a village. They got their Auntie D, Momma J, and I guess that Kēssa person. I don't know what she do, but we'll figure that out later. And the only nice thing I could ever say about his punk ass is that he loves them boys. He's not going to abandon them. And for the starting over part . . . trust and believe there's joy in it. I promise you."

～

The person that surprised me was Momma. When I told her what happened, she sat quietly for a minute as she listened to me crying.

"I know you're hurting, baby. He fucked up! But y'all got them boys, and they need they daddy."

"Really, Momma? So, I'm supposed to act like what he did was okay?"

"Naw, I'm not saying that. You did the right thing, kicking him out. He's lucky you didn't do more than that. All I'm saying is give it some time. He'll get some act right. But don't throw away the baby with the bathwater."

"Momma, what does that even mean?"

"That means don't throw away the whole relationship over one hoe." I couldn't believe that was the advice my mother was giving me.

Kēssa was right about one thing: being alone sucked. I missed being kissed, hugged, touched. Which led to me kissing Ricky one evening after work.

See what had happened was, he walked me out to my car after work like he usually did. I was leaning on the front of the hood of my car. We were talking about something. I have no idea what, but it was a good conversation because it was starting to get dark and everyone else had left.

"Dang, Ricky! We been out here a minute. I gotta go get my boys."

"True that. Alright give me a hug."

We always had a friendly hug here and there, but this hug was different. Our pelvises were pressed together, he was holding me tight with his head in the crook my neck, and I felt his desire for me. I allowed it to linger because I just needed to be held and it felt good to have his strong arms around me. But then out of nowhere, he kissed me. Ricky has nice, juicy lips and his kiss was tender, so I allowed it to continue. It's when he started laying me back on the hood of the car that I had to stop him.

"Okayyy . . ." I said, pushing him off of me.

"My bad. I got carried away. You don't know how long I've been wanting to kiss you, but you were with dude so . . ."

"No, I get it."

His attention was welcome. We started spending a lot of time together. We would take walks around the building at lunch some days. We made googly eyes at each other every time we made eye contact. I would go over to his apartment, and we would sit and talk about my issues with LaMar. He said encouraging things like, "You didn't deserve that. You're a good woman" and "You're too amazing to put up with that." We'd also talk about the many females that he "talked" to. I realized he had hoe tendencies, but that didn't matter. He was just a friend, and the only benefit was him making me feel good about myself since I couldn't find it within myself. As long as he didn't try anything, we were cool.

Ricky asked one day if he could come to my house to chill for a change of scenery. I told him no. I couldn't entertain the thought, even though LaMar was gone. I still felt as though it was our place and the thought of another man being there felt wrong. When I explained it to Ricky, he asked questions that made me think, such as if I was considering taking him back and would I be able to fully trust him again.

I didn't know how to feel other than broken. Though I walked around at work with a smile on my face, my heart hurt constantly every day. I continued wondering if it was somehow something I did wrong. Was I wrong for trying to push him to help take care of our family? Did I change in some way? Was I putting in enough effort to show my love for him? I know it wasn't a sexual thing unless you count the fact that I stopped doing oral when he wasn't working. But we still had sex whenever he wanted. Maybe she was giving him head. Was I too busy with work and the kids? Was it because I didn't take interest in hanging out with him and his friends?

My thoughts would then switch. How was it so easy for him to lay with another woman and come home to me, even if it was just kissing and touching? Here I am knowing he cheated, and I can't even let a man come into my house. And we're broken up.

I know I did everything I could to still be his woman and his friend. If he had a problem with anything, he could've talked to me instead of going to another female and lying to her and himself so that he could rationalize what he did. Hell, if that's what he wanted to do, he could've told me he was unhappy and moved out. But he had it good here. What did DJ Quik say? *Pussy, plate, and a place to stay.* There wasn't any excuse for what he did, and we both paid the price.

The nights he would keep the boys were so lonely. I'd walk into the house, and it was too quiet. No smell of food, no cheers from his video game, no weed smoke in the air. It made me miss him more. But I still wasn't speaking to him other than to say what was going on with the boys for the day. When we would talk, he would try to get me to let him come over or to meet him. I kept saying no. He would always make sure to end our interactions with, "I love you so much." I didn't reciprocate though. I was still in my feelings about the whole thing.

AFTER A COUPLE MONTHS OF HIM BEGGING FOR US TO talk, I gave in. It was Friday night, and my mom had the boys for the weekend. I had been watching TV but dozed off. My phone woke me up. I saw it was him. I didn't want to answer, but I did anyway.

"What?" I answered, trying to sound nonchalant and awake.

"Dang, it's like that? I just called to see how you are doing."

"I'm fine, LaMar."

"You don't sound fine. As a matter of fact, you haven't sounded fine in a minute."

"Whatever."

"Baby, are you ever going to hear me out? I promise not to come to you with no bullshit."

"Fine. Say what you got to say." I wasn't going to listen, but if it would get him to leave me alone, he could talk till his face turned blue.

"Not over the phone. I need to look you in the eyes so you can see how real it is."

"What is there to talk about, LaMar? I don't feel like talking." I sounded as dry as I felt.

"Please, could you come over here?"

"I'm tired, so I don't feel like going anywhere. The boys are with Momma, and I'm trying to relax."

"I know the boys are with Moms. She's the one that said to call you to see if we can work this out."

Hearing that made me almost roll my eyes clear to the back of my head. I should've known she was begging to keep the boys that weekend for a reason. I paused and had a long sigh. "I guess you can come over here then."

"I'm on my way!" He hung up the phone before I had a chance to change my mind.

I got up and made myself look good. No way was I going to let him see me looking a mess. I took off the hole-filled T-shirt and granny draws I had on and put on my red silk PJs and matching bra and panties. I left the top two buttons undone to let him get a peek at what he's been missing. Then I took my hair down (he always liked seeing my hair down) and put on just a little mascara and gloss. Sprayed on some Tommy Girl. I even went as far as to add some body glitter.

I heard the key in the lock, and for the first time in years I felt butterflies. I missed him. It had been a long time since he was here for more than just enough time to pick up our sons. And even then, I didn't let him come in. Still, I wasn't ready for him to come home. I thought to myself, *I should've took that key*. I sat up in bed, made sure my cleavage was showing as I heard him coming down the hall. I was pretending to read Stephen King's *Dolores Claiborne* like I wasn't anxiously waiting for his arrival. When he came into the room, I just looked up from my book and went back to reading.

"Hey, Toi," he said, smiling. I glanced up at him as he walked over and sat on the edge of the bed. "You look nice."

I know. You miss this don't you? I thought to myself but stayed silent.

"Are we going to talk or you just going to keep reading?"

I could tell he wanted to touch me, but he knew better. He had no idea that as soon as I smelled his cologne, I was turned on. I heard my momma's voice say, *"Closed legs don't get fed."* That's what I heard in my head, but the saying is "Closed mouths don't get fed." I was obviously past horny and started to regret letting him come over.

I set the book on the bed and looked at him.

"Talk about what?" I asked with a serious, straight face.

"Us! Me and you! Baby, I miss you so much!" He reached out for my leg. I moved it. "See, you won't even let me touch you!"

He stood up and started pacing, obviously bothered. It tickled me a little. He sat back down, scooting me over so he could get off the edge of the bed. He grabbed my hand tight so I couldn't pull it away. Lord knows I tried.

"Baby, please chill. Just listen. Please."

I let him keep my hand but looked away.

"Look at me. Toi!"

I looked at him and felt heat rising between my legs. *Why Lord?*

"I fucked up! No excuses. Wasn't your fault in any way because all you've ever done was held me down. I know you love me still. Say you don't."

"I know it had nothing to do with me, and I never said I didn't still love you. But what you did makes me wonder why I do. I'm working and taking care of you and the kids. So if you can do what you did and not think about that or think about our kids, what I look like still trying to hold you down? All a sorry man can do is keep a good one away. I deserve better." I proudly repeated my momma's words.

"You're right, baby. I haven't been the man you deserve. I get it now." He leaned his head to the side to look me in the eyes. "I got a job." He grinned.

"That's nice." I shrugged my shoulders. He'd had jobs before.

"I haven't been messing with nobody even though we haven't been together."

I wanted to believe that, but I didn't. "So now you're faithful. It's a little too late for that don't you think?

"Maaan . . ."

"Let me ask you this, since you want to talk. Why?"

"Why what?"

"Why'd you cheat?"

"Man, I told you. I was hurt."

"Oh, so hurt people hurt people. Why couldn't you come talk to me instead of running over there to her?"

"You know how I am. It's hard for me to talk about my feelings."

"Sounded like you were talking to her about how you felt about me with no problems."

"I don't know how you figure."

"She said you told her I was trippin' and that I didn't believe in you anymore. All you had to do is tell me that you were feeling that way. We could've talked it out."

"That's all I told her. It's not like I got all in my feelings like she was making it sound."

"I have another question then. How was it so easy for you to come and lay next to me knowing you had been with her? You were smiling in my face and shit. Better yet, did you have sex with her and then come home and have sex with me too? Did you at least wear a condom?"

"See, there you go!" he said, throwing up his hands. "What kind of question was that? Of course, I wore a condom! I wouldn't disrespect you like that! I only had sex with her twice. And only one of those times did I even come home. One time I spent the night over Malik's after it happened. Both times was after we had been fighting, so you and me weren't having no sex anyway."

"Oh, not wearing a condom is over-the-line disrespectful,

huh? Not you fuckin' someone else! I see. That makes so much sense!" I started to feel angry all over again.

"It was all bad! I was saying I wouldn't do that to you! I wouldn't put you at risk or take the risk of getting someone else pregnant!" he yelled, then lowered his tone. "I felt horrible that night I came home. I didn't sleep. I laid down on the couch because I couldn't lay next to you knowing what I had done. The sex wasn't even good. I ended it with her and that's why she called you."

"So you've said."

"It's true. You remember. I was coming home and staying home more at the time."

"Then the whole time before that was because you were with her?"

"No! I'm just saying . . . you overthinking the whole thing, per usual."

"And what's the point in tellin' me how good the sex was? So if she was putting it down you would've kept messing with her, huh?"

"Why you twistin' my words? I'm sayin' it wasn't that good because I felt like shit the whole time."

"Was that the first or the second time?"

"Both!"

"So, you had to do it the second time to see if you could shake that feelin' off?"

"No, I was drunk, and I shouldn't have even went over there."

"You got that right! Who else?"

"What?"

"Who else were you fucking? How many others were there?"

"Baby, it was just her. I didn't mess with none of them other females."

"How am I supposed to trust you?" I asked, feeling confused. "Every time you feel some type of way, you're going to go get someone else behind my back? I'm not living my life worrying if my man is out fucking around!"

"I know that. You won't have to worry. I swear on everything, I will never make you feel this way again. Ever!" He moved closer to me and took my hand again.

"I don't know if I can believe you." Tears filled my eyes.

I couldn't hide the pain anymore. As I started to cry, he pulled me to him.

"No, LaMar. I hate you." I cried harder and tried to push him away.

"I'm sorry, baby. Please, stop. I'm sorry. I love you. I swear I love you. She didn't mean nothing to me."

I stopped fighting and ended up crying in his arms.

Crying himself, he whispered, "I'm sorry. I'm so sorry. I never meant to hurt you. I love you so much. Please forgive me, baby."

I tried one last time to push him away, but he held on, and then he kissed me. It had to be the most passionate kiss he'd ever given me. The next thing I knew, my PJs were off. He was kissing my neck, making his way down to my breasts. He lingered there for a minute, giving attention to each one. I was saying "no" very softly because I couldn't make myself mean it. He was using my spot against me. I took a deep breath and let it happen. He worked his way down more, kissing every part of me on his way. He slid his fingers inside of me, then I felt his wet, warm tongue slide all over my clit. He licked me perfectly, with no hurry. Right before I came, he stopped. I don't know when he undressed. But when I opened my eyes, his slender body was climbing on top of me, hard dick included.

He looked into my eyes as he slid inside of me and said, "I love you."

Tears started to flow from me more. My body received him as if it was starving to feel his love again. My heart was crying "no" but my body was in control, and it reveled in the sensation of his touch and kisses. My skin drank in the warmness of his body pressed against mine. It felt good to have him inside me again. I let my mind go blank. Our bodies were once again in rhythm as we made love. He kept saying he loved me, but I still couldn't say it back.

Afterward, he held me in his arms. But the longer I laid with him, the dirtier I started to feel. What had happened didn't change anything.

"I think you should go," I said as I moved away.

"Really?" He sat up, looking at me, shocked.

"Yes. I need more time."

"But we just . . ." He stopped speaking and stared at me. I guess to see if I was serious. He took a deep breath and slowly got out of bed. "I can respect that. I'll go. I hope you heard what I said and felt that it came from the heart." He put on his pants and shirt. "I pray you'll give me a chance to make this better."

"Only time will tell how things will go. You have a lot of fixing to do."

"I'll do whatever it takes. Whatever it is you need from me. You need more time, you got it. No pressure. You need me to show you I'm keeping this job, you need to go through my phone . . . whatever you need."

I wished I had a list of things I needed. I had no idea how to explain it. How do you tell someone how to fix betrayal, hurt, and dishonesty?

"Be patient and show me I can trust you from here on out."

"I got you. And you'll see."

"You can show me better than you can tell me."

Chapter 13

Damn

LaMar

On the drive back to Pop's, everything played out again in my mind. I sure didn't want to leave. I felt as though I was back in there till she pulled that "you should go" shit on me. Man, I hated myself for hurting Toi like that. I swear it wasn't my intention. And I wasn't lying when I said that it was because ol' girl liked me and it seemed Toi didn't anymore. I mean, I knew I wasn't handling business like I should've been, but Toi had it. Wasn't like we were broke. I couldn't understand why she was trippin' so much. I was planning on getting another job but to keep it real, I wasn't in a hurry. I loved cooking but I was tired of working at all those damn restaurants. It took the fun out of it. But shit, I didn't know what else I could do. I only had two years of college and that was to play ball. I didn't learn nothing.

I still didn't understand why I couldn't go home. Okay, I had to be punished, I get that, and with the way she's been dissing me for the last couple of months, I was starting to feel like it was a forever thang. Which made me wonder if she might be entertaining someone else. I drove by the house more than a few times to see if I saw some dude over there. I can't even tell you how sick I was when I saw a car there one night. I sat outside for hours waiting to see who came out that house, and I was plottin' too. Whoever he was would've gotten hurt, but it was just Dena's bighead ass. I don't know whose car she was driving. That's the night I decided I loved Toi too much to keep messing up and went out and got my shit together.

Being away from them was the hardest thing I ever had to go through. I knew I would still get to see the boys whenever I wanted but, man, when I tell you Toi was giving me the cold shoulder that's an understatement. I was scared I made her hate me. The thought of that depressed the hell out of me. I started losing weight 'cause I couldn't eat. Wasn't sleeping good either. I stayed at Pop's mostly because there was too much going on at Malik's, plus Mia was still coming by trying to talk to me and the sight of her made me sick. The last time I saw her, she tried to apologize. I just walked off. She ran after me crying and shit, and I simply let her know what she did was fucked up and I didn't want to be anywhere near her. After a while, she stopped coming over there altogether.

Toi scared me with how she was acting when I first got over there, pushing me away and shit. But once she gave in, I knew it was just a matter of time. She was going to take me back. I simply had to wait it out. I felt the love pouring from her. And I seriously loved her too. I knew my actions wasn't showing it, but no woman had ever made me feel the way she did. She brought out a side of me that I didn't know I had, and she made me want to do better, believe it or not.

She doesn't know this but the first time we made love in a bed, I mean like really got to get it in, I cried a little. Nobody had ever made me feel that way. Hell, I don't think I had ever made love before. It was always bang, bang, bang. But she made me slow down and feel her. Not just her body but her kisses and tender touch. She showed me how to be gentle. And not only that, but I was also able to open up to her. I don't tell everybody about me being adopted and how my last girl left.

That's why I couldn't lose her over fucking with Mia. I don't even know why I lied about my situation. Mia was going to give me the pussy anyway. I mean she did suck my dick the first night we met. And I still don't know how you catch feelings after only getting the dick two times. I should've known she was crazy then. She kept blowing up my phone. I was done though. I hadn't talked to her in over a month when she pulled that shit with Toi.

Kēssa was the only one on my side. That damn Dena was always in Toi's ear. Just because her dude wasn't no good don't mean she had to put that shit on me. I wished Toi never met her. What happened to the well-spoke, white black lady Toi told me about? This Dena person was a nuisance.

On top of that, Momma Jewel was mad at me. I went to pick up the kids from her after everything went down, and she didn't say anything, disappointment all in her eyes. Then she reached in her purse, and I thought she was going to shoot me. I forgot I asked her for LJ's medical card. But I would've deserved it. I was so happy when she finally started talking to me again. And when she called me earlier that night saying she had the kids and for me to try to go over there and work things out with Toi, I just knew that was a sign from God that I was about to get my family back.

"Now, I'm gone help you this time, but you mess up again it's on you," she told me.

"Yes, ma'am. What should I do?"

"If she lets you come over, you need to take responsibility for everythang. Don't be over there talking about because she did this, you did that. What you did, you did because you wanted to."

"Yes, ma'am."

When Toi said I could come over, I thanked God all the way over there. And I did exactly what Momma Jewel said. And it worked, for a minute.

When I got to Pop's, I went to the back and fell back on the bed.

He cracked the door open. "Oh, it's you. I wasn't expecting you back. I thought you were getting back with Toi?"

"She made me leave."

"Damn shame you messed that up." He closed the door.

I laid there a while, mind racing. I didn't know what I was going to do, but I was going to do everything in my power to get my woman back.

Chapter 14

Starting Over

For the next several months, LaMar worked hard at getting back home. He kept the boys most of the week and on weekends, which kept him in the house and gave me some freedom to go out and have some fun. Dena, Ricky, and I all hung out and went out. I no longer felt lonely or depressed.

LaMar started to wine and dine me. He actually paid for everything. It wasn't like he was taking me on trips, but it was nice I didn't have to come out of pocket. We spent quality time together like we did when we first started. We enjoyed getting to know each other again. I was happy with the way things were. I almost didn't want him to move back in. I had freedom and wasn't worried about what he was doing, plus men were trying to get at me left and right. I wasn't interested, though it did boost my confidence. It was all good.

One day I got a call from Kēssa on my way home from work, asking me if I could stop by. I went over, mostly to see the girls. I played with them for a bit before she ran them off to their room.

"So, what's up? Why you ask me to come over here?" I asked.

She looked at the time. "Why do I have to have something major going on to have you come over here nowadays?"

"Bitch, I'm busy and tired. You know I like to go straight home when I leave work."

"I know, but I haven't seen you in a while. You always with that Cadonna, Kadeen, or whatever her name is. So, we don't kick it like we used to."

"Her name is Dena. And I'm not always with her."

"Like I said, whatever her name is. If you not at her house, she at yours, or y'all out somewhere. It would be nice if I was at least invited."

"Awww you're jealous!" I went over to hug her. "I'm sorry, sis." She looked at the time again. "Are you expecting someone to show up or something? Why do you keep looking at the time?"

"Girl, Devante on his way to pick them up." She smiled and rolled her eyes.

"Is he coming to pick them up or you?" I knew she was still sprung on him no matter how sorry he was.

"He comin' for them." She covered her smile which told me everything I needed to know.

She knew I couldn't stand his ass. He was the kind of dude who would be with a female and try to see if he could holla at her friends at the same time. Plus, we found out he was married. She was so damn blind that she refused to see how slimy he was.

He pushed up on me one time but knew never to do it again.

We were at a house party. Usually, Kēssa and I showed up everywhere together, but she told me to go ahead because she was waiting for her babysitter to show. LaMar had went somewhere with his brother Malik and left me at the party alone. I wasn't mad. We knew everyone there. Anyways, Devante came in, and when I saw him I went to a corner out of his eyesight—so I thought. He came into my corner talking about he needed to talk to me.

He was standing so close I could smell the weed and liquor on his breath. The corner I was in was kinda hidden and it was dark in there, which made me feel trapped and uncomfortable with him all up on me. What if Kēssa walked in? Hell, what if LaMar came back? If anyone saw how close he was to me, they would swear something was going on. I looked around but no one was paying any attention. He leaned in closer and shouted over the music.

"Where yo' friend at?"

"She's at home waiting for someone to come watch your child so she can get here."

"That's what's up!" He looked around. "You sholl is fine. I should've hollered at you instead of Kēss! You got body and face." He tried to put his hand on my hip.

I pushed his hand away. "You need to get out my face!"

"Oh, it's like that? You know you want me! I know how y'all talk, and I'm sure Kēss told you how I put it down in the bedroom. I bet yo' pussy taste like caramel candy!" He licked his lips and leaned in like he was going to try to kiss me.

I kneed him in his shit, pushed him over, and hurried out the corner.

"What the fuck wrong with you?" he growled, bending over in pain. "Bitch, that hurt!"

I didn't even look back when he called me a bitch. I felt disgusted. I never told Kēss. I couldn't break her heart like that. Besides, it probably would've come between our friendship. She believed everything his sorry ass said. I told her I saw him with another female all hugged up and kissing, walking around downtown one night, and she didn't talk to me for two weeks. All he had to say is it wasn't him and that I lied because I didn't want to see them together.

She didn't even find out he was married until after she had Keela. He said he didn't tell her because he was just so in love with her and that he wasn't with his wife anymore. They were just married on paper.

I told her a long time ago something was up with him. He never spent the night, she didn't know where he lived, and if she called after a certain time he never answered. She got mad at me about that too. So, there was no way I could tell her what he did.

Anyways, we talked and played with the kids until he knocked on the door. Kēssa hopped up so fast! Her excitement made me feel sick.

He came slinking his way into the house.

"What up, Toi! Haven't seen you in a minute! I see you still fine as evah!" He looked me up and down, making my skin crawl.

It bothered me that she never checked him on the way he always seemed to talk about how fine he thinks I am. I would've been done said something if LaMar said that to any female in my face. She just smiled.

"Hey," I mumbled. He knew I didn't like him. "Well, Kēss, I'm going to go since you have company now." I grabbed my purse off the table. I walked to the back and hugged the girls, who I was sure weren't going anywhere.

I walked back through the living room, and he was sitting at the table rolling a blunt.

"You don't have to run off on account of me." He watched me walk by, undressing me with his eyes.

"Yeah, I do," I said and kept walking.

Kēssa didn't try to stop me either. All that shit she was talking about us not spending enough time together and as soon as this creep came through, she saw me to the door.

"Okay, sis, let me know you made it home. Love you." She hugged me and practically pushed me out the door. Just rude. Oh well, I was ready to go anyway.

LaMar

I had been doing everything in my power to reassure Toi. I knew she was feeling the love. She even let me spend a few nights at the house. But I was tired of being in the doghouse, so I came up with this plan to cook for her, rub her feet, and put it down on her till she gave in.

I took the kids over to Momma Jewel's and had Kēssa call her over to give me time to get everything ready. I had her favorite music and food and I lit some candles. There's no way she was going to say no to me again.

Toi

I got home and there was LaMar's car in the driveway. I had no idea he was stopping by. I walked up to the front door and the smell of food welcomed me. I went inside and saw he had some flowers on the table—they weren't real but it's the thought that counts. He had candles lit, music playing. He walked out of the kitchen to greet me at the door.

"I hope you're hungry." He took my purse and set it on the couch. He was all dressed up in slacks and a dress shirt, got his hair cut and goatee shaped up perfectly. He led me to the dining room table.

"What's all this?" I smiled.

"It's been a while since I made you dinner. I wanted to surprise you." He pulled out my chair.

Oh, so this is why Kēssa had me stop by. She always had his back.

I sat down, and he ran the menu down. "We're having lemon pepper T-bone steaks, mashed potatoes, and a nice garden salad with no tomatoes and no onions of course." He laughed as he walked back into the kitchen to bring out our salads.

"This is so sweet!" I said, blushing. He brought out our plates and sat down next to me. "This looks good, LaMar."

"Thank you. I knew it would be something you'd appreciate." He leaned over and kissed me.

We enjoyed good conversation and laughed a lot during dinner. I couldn't help but smile at how consistent he had been the last several months. Working, taking care of our babies, giving me money for bills, taking me out—and he hadn't been pressuring me either. He was actually treating me like I meant something to him. Did I trust him? No. But I did believe he found him some act right. And I appreciated the fact that he was showing his maturity and taking responsibility.

After dinner, he took the dishes into the kitchen, grabbed my hand, and escorted me over to the couch.

"Now let me rub your feet."

He wasn't going to get an argument out of me. I took my shoes off, laid down, and threw my feet up on his lap. I closed my eyes, and let LaMar gently massage my feet, as D'Angelo's "Untitled (How Does It Feel)" took me away.

"Things have been so much better between us, wouldn't you agree?" he asked.

"Mmm-hmm."

"And you know it's been almost a year since I've been out the house."

"Yelp." I was still mostly listening to D'Angelo.

"Don't you think it's time I come home?"

"Mmm—huh?" I snatched my foot out of his hand and sat up.

"I'm just saying. I think I've proved myself enough to at least come home. Babe, I'm sick of being out there going from Pop's house to Malik's. I wanna come home and be with my own family. Besides, I know the boys would love that too. They miss me being here and seeing us together."

This wasn't a sweet gesture. This was a setup. "I don't know, LaMar."

"Please, baby!" He pushed me back, climbed on top of me, and kissed me. "Pleeease." He unbuttoned my shirt, going straight for my breast. "Please?" He kept whispering as he undressed me and proceeded to have his way with me on the couch. When he realized I was about to climax, he said, "You want me to come home, don't you?"

"Yes!" I whimpered. I would've said yes to anything right then. That's like asking yo' momma for money while she sleeps.

You'll get the answer you want, but you might get yo' ass whooped later.

After, as he held me in his arms, I still felt the need to make a point.

"Let me say this now that I'm in my right state of mind. You can come back but only on a trial basis. This doesn't mean you can't or won't be asked to leave again if things don't continue the way they have been. Capiche?"

"I'm not even worried about all that." He smiled from ear to ear and hugged me tight. "Thank you so much, baby!"

THE NEXT DAY WHEN I GOT HOME FROM WORK, I WENT into the room. The closet door was open, and I saw some of his things back in there. I didn't mean for him to come back immediately. I should've put a date on it.

While standing there in awe of how fast he was getting back in, the front door opened. I looked around the corner, and he was struggling to get through the door with an armful of stuff.

"You didn't waste any time moving back, huh?" I said with my eyebrow raised.

"What, and give you a chance to change your mind? Hell, naw! We doing this today!" He laughed.

I grabbed some of his things to help him take them into the room. "Where are the boys?"

"They're with Malik. He took them to the park to give me some time to get this done. You know he's happy to get his spot back to himself." Putting his things down on the bed, he said, "Can I have a welcome home kiss?" Instead of waiting for me to answer, he grabbed me and kissed me. "I can't wait for my first night back!" He smiled and smacked me on the ass.

I helped him get the rest of his stuff inside and put away. When we were done, we both sat down, looked at each other, and smiled. Honestly, I was only smiling because he was.

He left to get the boys, brought them back, and followed them inside.

"Mommy, Daddy in the house!" LJ shouted. LaMar put Ty down next to me on the couch and he jumped in my lap.

"I can see him, little boy," I said as he hugged my neck.

"Is he 'posed to be in here?"

"He lives here, so yes."

His eyes got wide and his mouth fell open. "He not live with Pawpaw and Uncle Malik no more?"

"Nope, I'm back here to be with y'all." LaMar picked him up into his lap.

"Yay! Daddy back home!" LJ sang, dancing around.

Ty was only two at the time, so he just sang *Dad-dy* because LJ did. He had no idea what they were happy about. Still, it brought such joy to be able to bring them joy. LJ followed LaMar around the house for the rest of the night. I guess to make sure he didn't go anywhere.

"LJ, I'm trying to cook. Can you let go of Daddy's shirt?"

He did but started pouting immediately. LaMar picked him up and set him on the counter.

"Daddy not goin' nowhere. I really am home. You want to help me cook?"

LJ nodded yes.

It was nice to be able to chill with Ty while he had LJ. Two little folks at once was a handful. And for the first time in a long time, we took turns bathing them and we tucked them into bed together. He stayed behind to read to them. It felt good to have him here with me again.

After getting the boys down, I showered peacefully, came out, and turned on the TV. Figured we could cuddle and chill. But as soon as he came out the bathroom, he turned the TV off.

"It's been too long since I've touched you. I'm not going to waste time pretending like I can watch anything but you on top of me."

"Boy, we were just together last night. What are you talking about?"

"Yeah, but that was before I came back. This gone be 'I'm back' sex."

He climbed into bed next to me and just stared into my eyes.

"Why are you looking at me like that?"

He pushed a curl back off my face. "You're so beautiful, sometimes I can't believe you're mine."

And once again, we became one.

Chapter 15

Celebration or Naw

I told Kēssa that LaMar moved back in but not Dena. I wasn't ready to hear what she was going to say. Kēssa was ecstatic and supportive.

"Now don't it feel better to have him home?"

"Of course it does. And the boys are so happy."

"I wish Devante would move in with us."

"Why?"

"Girl, I love when he comes over. And my girls would love if their daddy was around all the time. He helps a lot with them when he's here."

"When was the last time he was there long enough to help the girls and not just help himself to you? Did he take them with him the other day when he came by?"

"This not about me."

"That's what I thought." I knew he wasn't taking them nowhere.

"What yo' wanna-be best friend Shamena have to say? I know she mad."

"You know her name is Cadena. Or you could just call her Dena."

"Whatevah."

"I haven't told her yet."

"Wait, I know something she don't know? Wow!"

I avoided Dena coming over for a week. Every time she'd mention stopping by, I'd make an excuse. Imagine my surprise when Dena popped up at the house and LaMar answered the door.

"Ah, hell naw!" she shouted, pushing past him. "Where's Toi?"

"Why you come in here talking all loud?" he asked, closing the door behind her. "Good to see you too, by the way."

"I'm hoping I'm hallucinating." She opened and closed her eyes a few times. "Why are you here? Did you do something to her? Is she tied up in the back somewhere? TOI! Try to knock something over so I know where to look!"

"You funny."

"Auntieeee!" The boys ran and hugged her when we came out the back.

"Girl, what's wrong with you?" I asked, laughing.

"I came to check on you and the boys since you weren't answering my calls last night. I pray this wasn't the reason." She pointed at LaMar.

"Auntie D, Daddy no live with Pawpaw an'dem no mo'. Him live here again," LJ said, the little snitch. I just realized that shit started early on. Snitchin' became a habit for him.

Dena got down to his level.

"I see that, baby. Y'all take these toys back there and go play. Auntie needs to cuss out—I mean, talk to Mommy for a minute, okay?"

"Yes, ma'am." He happily took the bag and his little brother by the hand and headed to the back.

Dena stood, put her hands on her hips, and started tapping her foot as she stared at me, shaking her head.

"What?" I asked as LaMar came and stood next to me, put his arm around my shoulder, and kissed my forehead.

Dena gagged.

"You don't seem happy that we're working things out," LaMar said.

"She might've fell for the BS, but I see straight through you. You's a ho, you's gone remain a hoe. It's just a matter of time before yo' hoe ass mess up again."

"Damn, Dena! You said that like you don't like me or somethin'." LaMar walked off and smacked me on the ass on his way.

"Yeah, gone back there and play yo' game. That's all you good at doing anyway."

"Ask Toi about last night. I think I was pretty good at a few other things," he said before shutting the door.

She turned to me with fire in her eyes. "What the hell, sis?"

"What?" I said, going over to sit on the couch. She stomped behind me.

"You *know* what. Again, why is he here? Wait!" She jumped up and ran into the kitchen. "I know there's a jug of that shit in here somewhere." She started opening and closing doors.

"Girl, stop. It's not the water."

She came out the kitchen and sat back down next to me.

"Then it's something stronger. Hypnosis? Amnesia? Hoodoo? You know I heard if someone buries yo' panties in the yard you can't leave them. Let's go see if you missin' some underwear." She stood, but I pulled her back down.

"He wouldn't know anything about that. And why do you know anything about that?"

"Girl, there's all kinds of spells out there." She searched my eyes. "Yeah, I can see it in yo' eyes. You're not the same."

"I'm not the same after last night! Girl, LaMar has been putting it on me so good." I smiled from ear to ear.

"Too soon." She covered her ears. "The dick can't be that good. Oh wait, maybe I should ask Mia."

"Now that was a low blow, sis."

"I know. That's why I said it. I'm trying to break the spell.

Why are you tormenting yourself? You know he not gone do right."

"This is his last chance, I promise. I love him and I missed him. And the boys are so happy he's back."

"I get that, I really do. I miss Keyon's ass sometimes. Then I slap the shit out of myself and get over it. Or I get under to get over. What about Ricky? He's always up in yo' face. He sexy too. Why don't you get under him?"

"You know I don't want to mess with a dude at work. Besides, I love LaMar."

"I know. You've said that already." She rolled her eyes. "So, I guess you gone take care of his ass again."

"No, he's working."

"Yeah, for how much longer though? I can't believe this."

"It's going to be fine. You'll see. It's going to be different this time."

"Oh, I'm keeping my eyes all over this. And, bitch, I will use the words 'I told you so' when appropriate. I'm petty like that."

THAT WEEKEND WE ALL WENT OVER TO MOMMA'S. I thought she'd be surprised we were back together, but for some reason she didn't seem to be. LaMar probably called her already. She still had a word with LaMar and me.

"I'm glad to see y'all as a family unit again. I can tell the difference in my babies, and I see you are smiling again, Toi."

"Yes, ma'am." I grabbed his hand.

"Momma Jewel, I know I keep saying this, but I apologize. It won't happen again," LaMar said.

"It bet not," Momma said and opened her purse, which was lying on the table. She flashed her gun. "I told you once before, I will go to jail or hell for mines. I don't appreciate how you've been acting and treating her. You got one mo' time. Ain't no mo' chances after this. I'll make sure of that."

"Yes, ma'am," was all he could say.

Dena and Momma got along well, so she was now coming to Sunday dinner when Momma would have one. When I think about it, Dena reminds me of Momma when it comes to being overprotective of me. Momma threatens to cut or shoot people. Dena comes up with all kinds of wild ideas on how to take them out. I love both of them, but I just realized they both kinda crazy.

When Dena came in, she hollered out, "Momma J, where y'all at?"

"We in the kitchen and quit hollering in my house! Gone make my light bill go up."

Dena walked into the kitchen and rolled her eyes at LaMar. "Momma J, how in the world my yellin' gone affect you light bill?"

"I haven't figured that part out yet," she said, and they laughed and hugged.

"How am I supposed to enjoy yo' good cooking while Toi got that dog sittin' at the table?"

LaMar scratched the side of his face with his middle finger.

"Girl, hush and leave that boy alone," Momma said.

Dena and LaMar both got their little digs in all throughout dinner. I've never heard Momma have to chastise as much as she did that night.

"You two are like wax and water! Y'all just don't mix! Up in here acting like a damn lava lamp just back and forth all night! Y'all too old!" Momma said, frustrated. I mean what she said made sense, but it was the example she used for me.

"I'm sorry, Momma J. I don't like him and it's hard to pretend like I do. He dirty."

"Ain't for you to worry about. Toi gotta live wit'im, you don't. They have a family and it's best they stay together if they can. You stay out of it. You hear?"

"Yes, ma'am."

"Thank you, Momma Jewel," LaMar added.

"And you stop givin' her reason not to like you. She wouldn't be acting like that if you hadn't done what you did. Now, all y'all get out my house. Done got on my last nerve. And leave my babies."

Chapter 16

Here We Go Again

2003

The first year and a half after he moved back in, things were perfect. He wasn't going out. He still had his job, which was the longest he ever worked. The kids were happy, he was happy, and I was happy. But then . . . he lost his job.

I didn't trip for months after that. He did his stay-at-home dad thing as usual. I tried to focus on appreciating that. He wasn't going out, so I had to believe he was still trying to act right. I wasn't overjoyed about having to pay all the bills by myself again, although it wasn't a struggle. I just wanted my man to be a man.

I tried to keep my friends and family out of our relationship this go-round, but I started not liking him again and I didn't want a repeat of the last time. Maybe a little advice from someone on the outside looking in wouldn't hurt. I kept trying to act like I had confidence in him, but really, the longer he went without a job, the more I realized I didn't.

Kēssa kept her same energy. "Stay with him, girl. He's a good man."

Momma changed up. "Fuck it! Just let him go! Hell, I've never met a man that couldn't be consistent when it comes to working. What the hell is wrong with him? Why can't he keep his ass on a damn J.O.B?"

"I wish I knew, Momma," I replied.

"He's starting to get on my damn nerves with this shit now! I guess since you make good money, he expects you to take care of him too. What the fuck is he going to do when he gets bored, start cheating again? I told his ass this was his last damn chance. He done messed that up."

"I do worry about him doing that again. He has way too much time on his hands. LJ is in school all day now and Ty is in school half the day and daycare the other half. He's not going out and kicking it yet. I don't know what to do. I don't want to break up and have to do everything by myself. He's the one without a job, and I'm the one depressed behind it."

"First of all, do what by yourself?"

"Getting the boys back and forth, working, cooking, cleaning." I was exhausted thinking about it.

"Is he dying?"

"Momma, no! Why you ask me that?"

"Just because y'all not together doesn't mean he shouldn't do his part. He can do the same thang he did when you kicked him out last time. Hell, take him to court if for nothing but visitation. Lord knows you won't get no child support. Can't get blood from a turnip."

I completely forgot about how I'd handled things while he was gone. It wasn't *that* hard. I did all that and then some. Even enjoyed myself. Plus, I didn't have the stress of him not working or the worry about him cheating. Why the hell was I using that as an excuse?

"Okay, Momma. You're right."

"I know I'm right!" she yelled into the phone. I had to pull it away from my ear and look at it. "And number two, what I'm not going to allow is for my baby to be feeling all down and depressed over a *boy* who can't get his shit together! Y'all been on this roller-coaster for years now!" She muttered to herself. "Don't make no damn sense . . . a grown-ass man living off a woman with two of his damn kids." She resumed talking to me. "I'll tell you what. If you don't do something about it, I will!"

"Momma, what you going to do?"

"I'll have to cut 'im." We both laughed.

Of course, Dena had the same thoughts and feelings about it.

"First of all, I told you. I knew it was just a matter of time before the representative went back to sleep. They can only fight back the real nigga for so long. It's hard not being yourself."

"I'm starting to feel played for sure."

"I don't know why you waste your time with him! You could have whoever you want. Since I've known you, he's done nothing but bring you down. He won't work and thinks you his momma. Just because he gets to suck on yo' titty don't make him yo' baby." That was a deep one. "You can do better, sissy. I know he's a good dad, but he's not a good boyfriend. And he's broke! He ain't that damn fine either! Again, it must be the dick!"

Auntie was stuck on the same subject.

"I told you to move on already. What is actually keeping you with him without saying the kids?"

"Love?"

"Love don't love you enough to keep a job. Now, Yasin is handsome, tall with dark skin. He almost looks black. And he might be richer than Jabir. He has a whole castle in Dubai with servants and all. You wouldn't have to work yo' damn self, and he thinks you're beautiful. He's only four years older than you. You want me to give him your number?"

"How does he even know what I look like?" I asked, like I didn't know.

"I showed him pictures. How else? I'm trying to show you a different life, daughter-niece."

"Never mind, Auntie. Please don't give that man my number. I'll talk to you later. Love you." I hung up. She's as crazy as her dang sister.

I even confided in Ricky.

"He's not going to change. He doesn't know what he has. It's obvious he takes you for granted. I don't know why you took him back in the first place. You could've been with me. Do you think he's cheating again?"

"You know what, I don't even know."

"You didn't say no so he probably is. You need to drop that zero and get with this hero."

Everybody was right in one way or the other. That's why I was confused as to what to do. I tried writing down the good and bad things, and the good outweighed the bad, but the bad was so hard for me to accept. I felt disgusted every time I woke up to go to work and he was lying in bed sleeping like a baby. I did love him. I knew he loved me and the boys. I wasn't sure love was enough anymore.

Christmas came around and it was another year where I played Santa by myself. The gifts, whether for the boys or family members, I put both our names on, even though I was the only one who bought anything. I was truly fed up. He had the nerve to ask me to buy gifts for his dad, brother, nieces, and nephews. Really? It couldn't go on. When I tried to talk to him about how I felt, he didn't listen.

"Babe, you go job hunting today?" I asked after getting home from work one day.

"Man, it was so cold out. I stayed in, other than taking the boys back and forth."

"Oh, it's okay for me to get up and out in the cold, but not you?"

"You could've worked from home. You're the boss. I'm thinking about going back to school for something. I don't know for what yet. I'll figure that out by the spring or summer." He never even looked away from that damn NBA Live game.

I walked away, disappointed.

After Christmas and New Year's, nothing changed but the weather until I found out our landlord had decided to sell the house we were renting. I didn't want to buy it, so I began looking for a house to buy. I made good money, and my credit was straight. Why not get a piece of the pie? When I told LaMar what was going on, he shrugged it off.

"I'll move into whatever you find us to move into."

"You have a lot of time on your hands. I'll give you the price range and areas to look in and you can help me search."

"I don't know anything about doing all that."

"That's why I'm going to give you what you need to search it, and we can look at the pics or go see the houses together."

"I rather you do it."

A week later I had a couple of houses that I found to go look at. When I asked him to go and check them out with me, he still didn't want to.

"I wouldn't know what I was looking at," he said, sounding dumb.

"You'll be looking at a house."

"Naw, baby, you do that. Doesn't matter what it looks like to me."

"Look, I've done enough on my own!" I said, getting a little pissed. "You're a part of this family too! Makes no sense how I have to beg you to do anything! I have to beg you to find a job and now this? Sounds like I should be by myself, since I gotta *do* everything by myself!"

"Oh, you on one today, huh?" I was always either "on one" or "trippin'." "I was wondering when you were going to throw it up in my face about me not working! I told you, I'm going to go to vo-tech!"

"That's not going to help me put a down payment on the house. That's not going to help me pay bills, buy food, or whatever else is needed around here! I'm tired of feeling like I got three kids! I'm tired of having to take care of you! You're a grown-ass man and you haven't worked in months! And let's not forget the years you didn't work before that! We had to break up for you to keep the last job a year! What would happen if I lost my job, huh? Then what? Who's going to have my back and let me stay home chillin' and the bills still get paid?"

"That's not all I do." His tone came down a notch. "I go the store, cook, clean, and take the boys back and forth."

"I'm not saying that's all you do! Not once did I say all you do is chill! But you were able to do all that and work! Hell, don't act like I don't help take care of the home! I do all that right along with you, and I keep a job!"

"You just mad because I don't care about this whole house thing! I don't care! You aren't trying to move where I want to move, so I don't care!" he yelled, throwing up his hands.

"I'm going to need you to stop yelling. You know the boys are in there taking a nap." I brought my voice down. I was talking with a little extra bass, but I wasn't yelling.

"Yeah, I know. I'm the one who put them to sleep."

I ignored that little remark. "As far as moving where you want to move, why would you want to move to your daddy's neighborhood? Or should I say the hood? Didn't somebody get shot over there the other day? I'm not putting my boys in danger because you need some excitement."

"All the places you want to stay in is boring. That's why I don't care."

"How about quiet, clean, safe with good schools? You know, things parents care about."

"Yeah, so quiet I gotta worry about turning my music down before I turn into the neighborhood."

"I don't even want to hear all that noise."

"Yeah, I know. That's why we here now."

"So, you're tellin' me that you haven't enjoyed living here?"

"Not really."

"I'm sorry I don't feel comfortable around drama. And it's not cute to me to be ridin' around music bumpin' all loud. Can't even talk to each other. Ears ringing every time the music cuts off. Plus, it brings too much attention. It's dangerous."

"See, that's the problem. We're different. Most women I know would love to be seen in a car like mine. Maybe I'm too hood for you and you too boujee for me." He looked at me like I should be insulted. It used to bother me the way he said the word boujee but not anymore. I saw nothing wrong with wanting to live in nice places, around nice people. And if that's what boujee is, I'll be that. "I'm tired of trying to live up to your idea of a man. That's why I ended up messing with other females." As soon as it came out of his mouth, I could tell he wished he could take it back.

"Other females? That's plural . . . meaning more than one. You back to that again?"

"Baby, no. I'm sorry. I don't know why that came out like that. It's only been the one time. You already know. I wouldn't dare fuck up like that again."

"You got me fucked up! I feel like you just told on yourself."

"I'm saying it ain't like that. You know I haven't been doing anything. I've been home and not even going out other than to go over to Pop's or Malik's. You know that."

"What I know is that you *say* you're going to Dad's or Malik's, but I don't know shit. You met them other bitches at Malik's. Let me find out you fuckin' around again. I'm not going to be as nice about it as last time." I tried to stay calm. "You want some hood? Trust and believe there's enough in me to give you what you want." I guess he forgot who my momma was. "Don't worry, this will be the last time I ask you to do anything." I turned and walked away. He kept trying to get my attention as I was walking out the door. I kept walking. I was already late to meet the realtor.

The boys had woken up from their nap, so I took them with me. They'd seen a few houses, and LJ seemed to enjoy looking at them. He hadn't seen one he really liked yet though.

During the drive, I couldn't think about anything but that slip—*other females*. I decided then that once I finished the process to get my house, we were moving without him.

The day was long as we went from house to house, and we were all tired. I told the realtor we could look at one more. I followed him to the next spot and was surprised when we turned into this newly built neighborhood. All the houses were different and contemporary. Felt like we drove into a whole new world. Didn't look like Oklahoma at all.

We got to the house and pulled up.

"Mommy, are we going to live here?" LJ asked, eyes wide with excitement.

"Let's go inside and look and see if we like it."

The first thing I noticed was the circular driveway. Always thought that was fancy. It had a pretty garden area out by the mailbox with stone steps leading to it. The house had cream-colored bricks with black trim. It had two stone pillars that framed the front door, and I had never seen grass so perfect. The realtor called it a contemporary ranch-style home. I called it love at first sight. I couldn't wait to see the inside.

LaMar

I was slippin' for real. I couldn't believe I let that shit come out my mouth. Had I been hollerin' at a couple of honeys? Yeah. But it wasn't like I was kickin' it with them like that. I might've felt on a booty or two. Nothing too crazy. Fuck it, I'm lying. Since Mia, I have had sex with a couple other females, but shit Toi was trippin'. I know y'all knew I was going to say that, but it's true. And I figured what she didn't know wouldn't hurt her.

She was cool at first but around six months after quitting my job, she started that nagging shit again. Yeah, I quit. I told Toi I got fired, but that didn't happen this time. I went in that day and got tired of all that shit that comes along with being in the kitchen. The heat—I kept burning myself—and coming out smelling like food all the damn time. It wasn't what I wanted anymore and being there for so long made me realize it. My plan was to go to vo-tech and get into computers. Become a computer programmer.

Another thang that pissed me off is she stopped giving me head again. She didn't think I noticed, but every time I was unemployed she'd do that shit. She knew how much I loved head. She just didn't understand. But it was hard for me as a man to say what I was really feelin'. How you tell yo' girl you feel like you can't do nothing else, which in turn made you feel stupid and less than, without sounding like a little bitch?

And the house shit. I knew she was going to find a neighborhood that made me feel even more out of place. I'm a country boy. Most of the people in Hugo were black, and we all knew each other. People looked up to you if you could afford to put rims on yo' car and woofas in yo' trunk. That meant you were ballin'. But where we were staying there's no family, no friends. I've invited people to the house, and they didn't even want to come over. And the ones who did come agreed with me that they wouldn't feel comfortable being out there.

The first time Malik and Chris came, they had a few things to say.

"Bro. This is a nice spot. Quiet neighborhood. Everybody's grass cut. You feel white yet?" Malik said, clowning.

"Man, fuck you!"

"We been told you Toi is out of yo' league. She grew up with that rich auntie and shit. I mean, she cool but we can tell she don't fuck with us like that," Chris said, taking a seat.

"Yeah, bro, you remember how she was on the Fourth. The whole family was talking about how uncomfortable she seemed. You know I wish I would've got to her first instead of talking to that crazy-ass homegirl of hers. That bitch Kēssa got issues. At least Toi tries to blend in."

"She does try, I'll give her that. She just don't like being around a bunch of people she don't know," I said, defending her.

"With y'all moving out here, it seems as if she don't like being around her people." Chris raised his eyebrows.

"You crazy! My baby loves being a black woman!"

"I didn't say she didn't. She just don't love being around black people is all I'm saying."

"Naw, that ain't it. She's not used to being around the real. I saw her rollin' her eyes whenever someone would pull up with they music bumpin' or whenever one of the females would show up half dressed. Oh, and she damn sure was ready to go when that fight broke out," Malik pointed out.

"Yeah, she don't be feelin' that shit. And in a way that makes me glad that she's my babies' momma. I know my boys are gone be raised better than us. My sons not goin' to see the shit we saw. People getting shot, getting shot at, drug deals going down. I wish I hadn't been around half that shit myself."

"Yeah, he's turning white," Chris said, laughing. "Out here they have to worry about being lynched or somebody calling them a nigger."

"Nigga, shut up! You sound stupid! No, they don't!" Malik said, throwing a pillow at Chris.

"Yeah, Chris, you sound real stupid. It's not about black and white. There's plenty of black folk in this very neighborhood. Not like she moved us to some all-white spot. The people here are square is all. They go to work, to the grocery store, and home. They sit down and eat dinner and shit. Nothing we experience fo' sho. It's simply boring family life. We too young fo' that."

"Mar, don't listen to him. Ain't nothing wrong with wanting better fo' yo' kids. I'm glad LJ and Ty will never experience the street life. Shit, my babies' mothers are all chicken-heads. Livin' on Section Eight and food stamps, none of 'em want to work, all they want to do is smoke weed, drink, and run the streets. I gotta worry about them bringing men in and out, people fighting and pulling guns on people in front of them. One of them had some dopeboy living with her, sellin' out the house where my kids lay their heads. I had to go over there and regulate that shit. Not saying all women who needs assistance are like that, but the ones I messed with are. With Toi, you'll never have to worry about none of that. And though we clown you about it, I can see a change in you. You're not sellin' weed no mo', you talkin' about going back to school fo' computers and shit. I'm proud of you, bro."

"Thanks."

I knew at the time Toi was definitely doing the right thing for our little family. Didn't mean I had to like it. After a while she started buying me clothes I know she didn't think I was going to wear. Fuckin' button-up collared shirts and shit. Talkin' about for interviews. She was trying to change me into some square-ass mutha fucka but I wasn't going for it. Next thing she'd be trying to put me in ties and some ugly-ass Stacy Adams shoes. She needed one of those white-collar bruthas. And deep down inside I knew that's what she deserved. That wasn't me. And I wasn't sure if it ever would be me. Maybe I should've let her go because I didn't want to grow up yet. I wanted to drink, smoke, kick it. Get some new booty from time to time.

I didn't mind takin' care of my kids. I love the hell out of them. But family life . . . I wasn't ready for it. We've been together for a long time and was too young for that type of commitment. But I really didn't want to lose Toi. I loved her with all my heart. Maybe in five years I would've been able to settle down and chill but at the time there were just too many fine bitches out there and I wanted to sample a few.

Chapter 17

Boy, Bye

I would've never guessed buying a house would cause so much stress and paperwork. I had to gather bills and show proof of income just to apply for the first-time homeowner's loan. Then, once all that was done and approved, it took another four months to find a house I wanted to make my forever home. The boys and I fell in love with that house in the newly built neighborhood, and imagine my excitement when the seller accepted my offer. I've never felt so much happiness in my life. But still, I hated the process and having to do it alone made me not want to be with LaMar that much more. He didn't go look at not one house with me. Therefore, he had no idea where the new house was. He didn't even ask. But enough about then. That's all in the past.

This is now.

We're moving tomorrow and I haven't said a word to him about it. I get home from work and per usual, he can't wait to get out the door. I don't even trip because as far as I'm concerned, we're done anyway. Hell, I even give him twenty dollars for gas. The last dime he'll ever get from me. He doesn't even come home till three a.m. and I pretend to be asleep. I'm only awake because I'm excited yet nervous as to how things will go tomorrow.

I usually leave before he gets up to go to school, so he woke me when he woke up.

"Hey, did you miss your alarm or something? It's after eight."

"No, I'm going to do some work from home today. I'm tired. I don't feel like going in."

"You want to get the boys dressed for me since you're here?"

"No. Do what you usually do," I say and turn over.

"Man, you can get up and help! Shit, I'm tired as hell!"

"You wouldn't be so tired if you hadn't stayed out all damn night."

"I'm not goin' to sit here and argue with you." He gets out the bed mumbling something. He makes sure to make as much noise as possible and turns on every light he can, which is such an asshole move. When I get up in the morning, I make sure not to disturb him. It's not like I get to sleep in every day. But since he's in his feelings, he's going to make sure I don't sleep in today either. That's alright though, because I'm just waiting for them to leave.

"Mommy?" Ty taps me all quiet and sweet.

"Yes, baby."

"Daddy said for me to ask you to help me with brushing my hair right. He said he's doing bruther's hair and we runnin' late." I sit up in bed and now I'm mad. He purposely sent my baby in here. He's getting so big. I can't believe my baby is almost five.

"Come here." I brush his hair, get me some kisses, and he runs out of the room. LaMar tells the boys to hurry up, and I can hear them running through the house. The front door opens, and he says, "Tell yo' momma bye."

"Bye, Momma! Love you!" the boys holler.

"Love y'all too!"

The door slams and I spring right up out the bed. I watch out the window as he gets the boys into the car and backs out of the driveway. I run into the room and text Momma and Dena that he's gone and then quickly get dressed. I didn't hit Kēssa up because I haven't told her what I was up to. I don't trust her not to say anything to LaMar. She's always trying to keep us together. If she knew I was moving without telling him, I'm almost sure she would say something to him.

I tie my hair up, pull the hidden boxes from my closet, the attic, and from under the bed, and get to work. We have three hours before the movers get here. Once I get the boxes ready, I decide to start in the kitchen since that stuff will be the hardest to box up. I'm wrapping glasses in newspaper when the doorbell rings. I look out the peephole and it's Dena. She has the biggest smile on her face I've ever seen.

"Hey, sissy! What a beautiful morning God has given us on this day of leaving LaMar! I mean moving!" She sticks her arm out, holding a cup of coffee. "I brought you libations to help move things along today."

"I got yo' libations! Get in here." I take the cup. "Thank you, though. I need this after the morning I had." She follows me into the kitchen.

"What he do?"

"Girl, he saw me sleeping in, woke me up, and asked me to help him get the boys ready like he don't do that every morning. When I told him no, he made sure I didn't get to go back to sleep. Even had Ty come in the room to ask me to do something."

"That's okay! We leaving this morning!" Dena says, trying to sound like Scarface. "Where do we start?" She glances around the room.

"In the kitchen."

We turn on some music, then wrap and box.

Momma walks in. "Hey!"

"Hey, Mommy!"

"I see y'all are making some progress already in here. You ready, ready?"

"Yes, ma'am." I stop to hug her.

"Heyyyy, Momma J!" Dena dances from behind the counter to hug Momma as well.

"Girl, why you smilin' all crazy like that?"

"It's such a beautiful day is all," Dena says, dancing back into the kitchen, snapping her fingers to the music.

Momma shakes her head. "Toi, I don't know about this chile. What you need me to do?"

"Can you go into one of the boys' rooms and start packing up their stuff?"

We work like crazy. The closer it gets to time for the movers to show, the more we start throwing things in boxes. We get everything that I'm taking packed up, and the movers arrive right on time. I show the movers to the boys' rooms first so they can start loading the big stuff. We help them load the boxes. Once we got the first load in, everyone follows me to the new house. This will be the first time Dena and Momma get to see it and I can't wait.

I pull into my circular driveway and help the movers back the truck in. I open the door to the house with Momma and Dena right behind me.

"Oh my God, SISSY!" Dena shrieks when she walks in. "This is so bomb! This place is huge and you in this boujee-ass neighborhood. Girl, you goin' to fit right in here."

"Shut up, D."

"No, I'm saying this is beautiful! You deserve this." She hugs me.

I look around for Momma. She's walking around in awe. "I love these high ceilings and crown molding. And the fact that no one else has ever lived here makes it that much betta."

"Y'all go look around. I'm going to show the movers where to put stuff."

After their self-tour, we get back to work unloading. I let the movers go, and we go back to grab some more boxes. We load our cars with the last of the things. I give Momma the key so they can go ahead of me to the house, and I stay behind to do a little cleaning. I go from room to room vacuuming, sweeping, and dusting. As I work, I can't help but think of how many joyous memories we're leaving behind. LJ outside chasing birds or playing basketball with his dad, the little hoop attached to the door. Ty saying his first words and taking his first steps. That one Christmas Dena and LaMar got along, when they played spades on the same team. Dena says she doesn't remember that because she was drunk. The love that was made in this bed I'm leaving behind for him. Along with the couch and loveseat. I bought new stuff because I can't take any of this into my new life. I have to have a completely fresh start.

I finish cleaning and slowly walk out. Before closing the door, I look around one last time knowing that my life will never be the same. I shut the door and lock it for the very last time. I get into the car and cry. This heartbreak hits different. I really do love LaMar, and I hate he doesn't seem to love me back.

I finally pull myself together and go back to my new house. When I get there, Momma and Dena are already unpacking boxes, drinking wine, and laughing about how frantically we were moving. Like we didn't have a few hours before LaMar came home.

"I almost fell a couple of times I was moving so damn fast!" Momma says, chuckling.

"Momma J, I don't know why I kept looking around like he was going to pop up and start wiggin' out!" Dena declares.

"Hey, y'all." I walk in and notice three glasses filled with wine. "I see you found my wine and wine glasses already."

"Yelp. Opened all these boxes until we did. You got a glass over here too." Momma takes a sip of hers. She and Dena look at each other and laugh. I wish I felt the joy they were feeling for me. I appreciate their support, but they have no idea how hard this whole thing is for me. But I grin, take my glass of wine, and get to work.

LaMar

I come home and Toi not even here. Acting like she was going to work from home. She could've got up and helped me this morning. She knew I was hung over. I throw my keys on the table, and something feels off. The TV is gone. *Did we get robbed?* I hurry into the bedroom. My TV and PlayStation is still here. That's a relief. I check my games and they all still here. What she do with the TV? I go back in the living room and look around. Some of Toi's little trinkets are gone. The vase her momma gave her for Mother's Day. Where she move that to? Pictures of the boys and her are gone. The ones with me and the boys . . . still here. Shit is weird. No telling what she up to.

I shrug it off. Don't nobody break into a house and steal certain pictures, trinkets, and a TV. I'll just ask her about it when she get back.

I go into the kitchen and open the fridge and grab a jug of water. I turn and open the cabinet to get me a glass and there are only two glasses in here. *What the fuck!* I open each of the cabinet doors and there is stuff missing from all of them. The plate set Dena got her for her birthday . . . gone. The boys' cereal . . . gone. *Huh?* Wait.

I run back in our room—more pictures missing. I go into our bathroom—her products are gone. I open her closet door and all her clothes are gone. I open mine and everything is in its place. This don't make no sense. I know she didn't—

I run to my boys' room and all they shit gone! Beds and all! *What the fuck?*

Toi

I pretty much down my wine and Dena pours me another glass. I turn on some music and we get a pretty good flow going in the kitchen. I hear a low buzz and realize my phone is ringing. I check it and I have five missed calls. I look at the time, and it's almost three thirty in the afternoon. Before I can check to see who called so many times, my phone starts ringing again and it's, of course, LaMar.

I turn the music down. "Hey, y'all! Shhhh! It's LaMar." I give it one more ring before answering. "Hello?"

"What the hell is going on?" he screams in my ear, almost busting my ear drum.

I pull the phone away. The way he said that reminds me of Mr. Biggs when he caught ol' girl with R. Kelly. I almost laugh and sing, "Baby, wait let me explain," but that's the wine talking.

"You need to calm down," I say instead.

"Why is all y'all's stuff gone, but my stuff still here?"

"Because we moved."

"Oh, so y'all moved without me?"

"You said you didn't want to live in the boring neighborhood I picked, right? I figured you'd want to find you somewhere exciting to stay."

"That's what's up. You know what, I don't need this shit! Don't worry about me! Just make sure I can get my boys whenever I want to!"

"I'm not worried. I would never keep the boys from their dad. You don't have to pick them up today though. Let me know when you get settled." He hangs up in my face.

"That went well," Momma says, and again we laugh.

I'll admit I feel bad for him after hearing the hurt in his voice. That was a sneaky thing I did.

LaMar

Toi got me fucked up! I'm so mad I don't know what to do! I'm not gone let this slide! She gone see my face! I'm about to go over there! That's going through my head when I hang up, but then I realize I don't even know where this new house is. Fuck!

I just flop down on the couch. I can't believe she'd do this to me. She promised she never would. She knows how I feel about people abandoning me. My momma did it. She passed away, and I ended up being adopted. My last girlfriend did it when she up and moved to New York. Now this. As I sit silently, I can't help but cry. What did I do that was so wrong to where I deserve this? Anything but this. She doesn't even know about half the times I messed around. Even though I'm not working, I'm going to school. What more does she want?

Hell, I've even been thinking about asking her to marry me. All she had to do is wait a few more months for me to finish Votech. They help people get jobs in the field they went to school for, so that wouldn't have been but another month. After I started working, I was going to buy her a ring. At least start paying on one. Now she done messed all that up.

I knew I should've come home during lunch instead of hanging out with ol' girl. Don't trip, I wasn't going to do nothing with her, but Toi has been on one again lately. Hell, she completely stopped giving it up at all. She has never told me no when I wanted some. But that's all I've been hearing since that "other females" slip-up I had. I should've known then she was up to something. I even thought maybe she was cheating, but I know better than that. That girl loves me too much.

If I would have come home, I probably would've caught her ass too. I bet that damn Dena was over here helping, just smiling and shit. Toi leaving me like this was probably her idea because I know my baby. She wouldn't do this.

I call Kēss. She'll know where to find her. "Hey, Kēss! What's up with yo' girl?"

"Who, Toi?"

"Yeah! She left me!"

"Huh? What you mean?"

"I mean she moved to her new spot and didn't even discuss it with me! She left all my shit here!"

"That's crazy!"

"Oh, so you gone act like you didn't know nothing, huh?"

"I didn't! She didn't even tell me she decided on a spot, I swear! I can't believe she did all that and didn't tell me! I bet that dang Camena Ca-whatever-her-name-is knows! I'm 'bout to call her!"

"Yeah, that Dena is definitely in on it. Do me a favor, find out where she at! I'm trying to go over there and talk to her ASAP! And try to play it off so she don't know I called you."

"I got you."

Okay, lil sis is on the case. I feel a little bit calmer knowing Kēssa will call back soon with some info. I flop back on the couch and fire up a blunt. I'm so stressed I can't think straight. Why did she leave the couch and bed and shit? I guess she didn't need it. Now I got to figure out what to do with this shit. And what am I supposed to do now? I can't stay here. They selling this place. I don't want to stay with Momma. She still tries to run my life. Always wanting to make decisions for me like I'm some little kid. I guess I could stay with Pops or Malik again. I'm sure they tired of me even though they've never said anything.

I know one thang—if she thinks she's going to keep the boys away from me, she has another thing comin'! Those are my sons, and I'm going to be a part of their lives no matter what she do.

Let me stop thinking about this shit. I don't know why I'm acting like a little bitch. This is temporary. Toi just needs a minute to stop trippin' and realize she needs me. I'll give her a few months till she comes to her senses. I'm just gone take this time to do me. I'm not gone to be all perfect like last time either. Last time I left them females alone and got my shit together. I had to beg her to take me back. This time I'm gone to sit back and wait for her to start missing me. She did me wrong this time. She should be begging me to come back.

Toi

Kēssa calls. "Hey, sis, what you doing?"

"Nothing." Mind y'all, I hadn't heard from her in a couple of weeks, and she never calls me when I'm at work. She would normally at least text first and ask me to call her when I can. I'm sure she has heard from LaMar by now.

"Oh, you workin'?"

"No." I'm going to keep my answers simple.

"Oh . . . umm, where you at?"

"I'm at home. What's up?"

"Nothing. I was just seeing what you were doing."

"Toi, where you want me to put this?" Dena asks. *Damn!* I know Kēssa heard that.

"Who was that? Madena?"

"Her name is Dena. Stop doing that."

"What?"

"Sayin' her name wrong on purpose."

"Anyways, what she doing over there?"

"We chillin'."

"Toi, you want me to put this in yo' new room?" Dena asks, holding up a painting.

"Yeah, you can put that in there."

"I think it would be cute to hang in yo' new bathroom," Dena says.

"Okay, just put it in there then." I just want her to shut up for a minute. Why she gotta label everything new?

"What she mean by new room, new bathroom? I thought you were at home."

"I moved, Kēss," I confess, rolling my eyes.

"Huh? You moved into your new house? Today?" she asks, trying to act surprised. She has no skills. I can see right through her.

"Yes."

"Why didn't you call me? I would've helped you move."

"I don't know. I didn't think about it."

"But you thought to have her come help. I see how it is. Anyways, how LaMar and the boys like the new house?"

"The boys love it. LaMar hasn't seen it yet."

"That's crazy. So umm, I can come help y'all. I can't wait to see it! What's the address?"

"Toi, come here!" Momma calls out.

"Let me call you back, Kēss."

"Is that Momma J?"

"Yeah, she helped me move. I'll call you back," I say and hang up the phone.

LaMar

I'm excited as hell when Kēssa calls back. "What's up, sis? Where she at?"

"You know she had the nerves to say she didn't think to call me to help her move but she got Momma J and that girl over there helping her."

"Bump that. I don't care about that right now. What's the address?"

"I asked, but Momma J called her and she said she'll call me back. She wasn't even going to tell me she had moved. She was acting like she was just at the house chillin'. I don't know why she doin' me like that."

"So, you didn't get no info?"

"Not yet. She's going to call me back."

"Fuck!"

"Chill, big bro. It's going to be alright. You know how Toi is. She mad at you one minute and kissin' yo' ass the next. She loves you. She not going nowhere."

"I don't know, sis. This feels different. There's been a lot of tension and distance between us lately. I'm not going to lie, I'm a little worried."

"You been around her too long. Over there overthinking. I'll call you when she calls me back and we can both go over there."

Once it starts getting dark and she hasn't called back, I give up. I'm just going to sit here and smoke myself into oblivion.

Toi

I didn't bother calling Kēssa back. I know when she's trying to set me up for failure, and I ignored her every time she called or texted. Later, I let her know where we are and made sure to stress that if she tells LaMar where I am, we not going to be friends anymore. I know it's killin' her not to say nothing, but she knew I wasn't playing with her ass and really she just wanted to be included. She cares about herself way more than LaMar.

I had Momma go get the boys and she's keeping them at her house so that I can get the house in order with the help of Dena and Kēssa. I want to make sure Ty and LJ's rooms are ready when they get here. Both the boys loved this house when we came to see it. They understood we were getting a new house; therefore, they won't be surprised about that. They will be surprised that I picked the house they wanted and how I hooked up their rooms.

I love our new house too! It is so beautiful. Four bedrooms, huge kitchen with black marble countertops. My room is on the other side of the house from the boys' rooms and the guest room. What did the realtor call it? Split bedroom floor plan. They have their full bath and I have mine. My tub is my favorite part. I have a black Japanese soaking tub, and the water comes out like a waterfall from the wall with the jacuzzi jets. I now have a large, black, U-shaped sectional and a big seventy-inch TV in both the living and family room. There are mirrors and bling everywhere. My bedroom is huge with a sitting area and a closet/dressing room. My headboard is tall and black button-tufted upholstery with faux crystals and chrome-toned accents. My mattress is a Cali king Beautyrest Natasha plush pillow top. Say that three times. I get sleepy looking at it. The dining room has a beautiful modern crystal chandelier over my silver and black dining room table and chairs.

I'm doing a SpongeBob theme in LJ's room. He loves him some SpongeBob. He's basically going to be sleeping in Bikini Bottom. I found these wall stickers of SpongeBob and Patrick along with some jellyfish, and they all glow in the dark. I can't wait for him to see it! Ty's room is painted in pale blues and beige. Ty doesn't have a favorite cartoon, but he has a favorite color: blue. I slapped some of those glow-in-the-dark jellyfish on his wall too.

The house doesn't have much of a front yard, but the back-yard is pretty and big. I have a guesthouse in the back that I'm dubbing the Toibox. It has a spacious living room, a kitchenette and bathroom, and lots of windows to open it up. A great place to chill and hang out that has heat and air. There's also a lovely flower garden, which is going to be Momma's favorite spot. The boys have their play area with a swingset and room for a trampo-line. Most definitely the forever home.

My first night, I climb into my new tub and lay back, letting the warmth of the water take me away. The peace of it doesn't last long because the pain from ending my relationship kicks in, and I try using the water to hide my tears. The water turns cold and my hands and feet wrinkle before I decide to get out. All cried out, I dry off, put on one of his oversized T-shirts, and crawl into my new bed. Before I know it, I drift into sound sleep.

IT'S A BEAUTIFUL SATURDAY MORNING, AND I WAKE UP so refreshed that I find myself humming for no reason. I have Dena and Kēssa coming over in a little bit to help finish things up. They haven't met yet, so this should be interesting. Kēssa always purposely gets Dena's name wrong. Dena forever refers to Kēssa as my used-to-be best friend. Can't we all just get along?

Chapter 18

Girls Just Want Peace

Dena shows up first and let's herself in. "Sissy, I'm here!"

I'm in LJ's room putting the finishing touches on his bed. I walk down the hall to greet her, and she holds up a bottle of my favorite wine called Twisted Sisters.

"There you are. This house is too big for me to run around here looking for you. I brought you something," she says.

"Now you know I always appreciate some of that Twisted Sista. Thank you!" We hug.

"And you know I always plan on getting twisted with my sista," she says, laughing and sticking her tongue out. "Looks like you've got a lot done already."

"Girl, my bed is so bomb, I had a lot of energy when I woke up this morning. I started working and haven't stopped." I smile at my progress.

"Well, show me where to roll the blunt then. You know I don't want to mess up anything or get weed dust all over your brand-new, beautiful floors." We walk into the kitchen and sit at the breakfast counter.

"You can roll there, but no smoking in the house. That's what the Toibox is for."

"Dang, okay. I'm not mad at'cha, but what the hell is a Toibox?" I walk her over to the patio door and point to the guest-house in the back. "Well, what do we have here?"

"You'll see when we go out there. I got it hooked up, too."

"Okay, so after we hit this then you can tell me what you need me to do."

"Before Kēssa gets here I want to give you this emergency key to the house." I hand her the key.

"Oh, shoot! I get a key to the mansion! I can bring my dudes over here and everythang!" She excitingly adds the key to her key ring.

"No. It's only for emergencies. Don't be using my key to come and go as you please, and you sholl bet not bring nobody to my house."

"Girl, I'm just playing with you. I would ask you first anyway. But for real, thanks for entrusting me with this."

The doorbell rings. "That's probably Kēssa." I turn to walk to the door. "I don't know why she didn't just come in."

Dena grabs me by the arm. "Hold up. She hasn't been here yet, huh?" She carefully places the blunt on the counter. "Let me get it. I've been wanting to meet her."

Dena runs over to the door and pushes it open. "Can I help you?"

"Um, is Toi here?"

"We don't sell toys here." They both stand looking at each other, blinking slowly. "Girl, I'm messing with you. I'm Dena. Toi's *best friend*. Come in." She steps aside and allows Kēssa to walk through the door.

"Oh, I've heard a *little* about you. I'm Kēssa, Toi's *actual* best friend. Since childhood. We're basically sisters." Kēssa looks Dena up and down. "I know you heard about me, though."

After a few minutes of silence, slow blinking, and looking each other up and down, they hug.

"Y'all get on my nerves! I thought y'all were about to square up or something." I hug Kēssa and we all head for the back to the Toibox.

When I unlock the door, Dena for some reason lit up. "This is niiiice! We gone smoke in here? Are you sure?"

"Yelp! This is the kick-it spot." I look around, brimming with pride.

"Girl! It's so roomy! Look, it even has its own bathroom and little kitchen," Kēssa adds, going into the bathroom to look at it.

Dena sits down in a few different places and finally settles, bouncing around.

"Okay, so when we come out here, this my spot. I can see out the door and that window over on the side. The table is close so I can roll. There's good lighting here. Yelp, this my spot." She sounds like a little kid.

"What happens if somebody sits in your spot, Dena?" Kēssa asks.

"I'm gone politely tell them to get they ass up."

"Yelp, Toi told me you were crazy."

"I'm not crazy. I don't know why she keeps telling people that. I'm real, there's a difference."

"Well, you sound crazy." Kēssa sits down next to Dena. "Can I get you to fire one of those up please?" She points to the blunts on the table.

"Say less." Dena picks up two blunts, puts them in her mouth, and lights them both. She hands Kēssa one. "If you're anything like Toi, you don't need a whole one. Y'all can share that."

After passing the blunt a few times, Kēssa says, "Damn, Dena, what the hell you put in that blunt?" She slouches down and lays her head back on the couch.

"Weed," Dena says, laughing and laying back herself.

"That shit got me gone. How we supposed to do anything?"

"Like this." Dena puts her arm up and quickly drops it back down. "You right, we fucked up. We're going to have to sit here and chill for a minute." We all laugh.

"So, Toi, what you going to do about you and LaMar?" Kēssa had to ask. I was wondering when one of them would bring that up.

"Girl, I'm so done. He's never going to grow up, and I'm tired. I'm gone do me."

"She doing what she supposed to do with him—leave him alone!" Dena adds.

"I hope you're ready for this single life. I promise it's overrated. I've been trying to find a man for years and still don't have one worth talking about," Kēssa says.

"You don't need no damn man all the time, Toi! Girl, you should take this time to figure out what you want, whether that be with or without a man. Hell, you might want a woman, I don't know," Dena says.

"Not me. I'm strictly dickly, thank you very much."

"Be single. If you want company, any man would be happy to give you his time. Date and have some fun. Or not. You's free!" Dena says.

I nod my head in agreement.

"Doing it by yourself is hard and lonely. I want someone to lean on, someone other than the kids to love me. I need a man!" Kēssa says.

Dena sits up, grabs another blunt, and lights it. She looks over at Kēssa with a look of pity. "Damn, that's sad! I'm sorry, Kēssa, but what you *need* is to love your damn self! I don't know your situation, but if you're having a problem with keeping a man or getting a good one, that's probably why. You *need* one. Self-love and self-confidence is the key to happiness, not no damn man! A man is the key to kids or an orgasm. And some of them can't get that right." Dena blows smoke toward Kēssa. They might fight yet.

Kēssa fans the smoke. "You can say that because you don't have kids. And I don't understand how needing some affection means I don't love myself. Hell, I love me!" Kēssa answers back, talking with her hands and neck.

"If you say so. When I left Keyon, I never looked back. I've been having the time of my life by my damn self!" Dena dances around in her seat.

"Kēss, I'm tired of playing games with him. And I don't want my boys thinking that's how a man is supposed to be in a relationship. Him laying up in here not working, cheating. It's just too much, and I don't want to continue to deal with it."

"He only cheated once—"

"Lies!" Dena shouts.

"You don't know, Dena." Kēssa frowns up at her.

"I know if you see one roach, there's probably a thousand more in the wall."

"How we start talking about roaches?" Kēssa asks, looking at me.

"What she's saying, Kēss, is that if I caught him once there's probably others I have no idea about. And I thought that when he had his slip-up."

"What slip-up?" Kēssa asks.

"We were arguing about going to look at a house and he said, 'that's why I messed with other females' or something like that. The only thing I hear over and over in my head is the 'other females' part—plural. He tried to say he didn't mean that but something in my gut told me that was the truth."

"Now I see why he says you be trippin'." I can't believe Kēssa said that. I look at her like I don't even recognize her. "I'm saying, sis. People say stupid stuff when they fight. He probably didn't mean it."

"Why are you friends with her? Nothing she says makes any sense." Dena looks at me for answers.

"Dena, that's not nice."

"And neither is her thought process. Girl, what is wrong with you?"

"What? Haven't you ever heard of the benefit of the doubt?" Kēssa responds.

"Haven't you ever heard that she has been approached by bitches at the store and seen him with a hoe in his car?"

"The girl at the store said nothing happened. And he told her who was in the car."

"Toi, can you look up the *Guinness Book of Records* and see if Kēssa is listed under the most gullible bitch ever, please?"

"Fuck you, Dena."

"Kēss, don't say that! Dena, really that's not cool."

"My feelings aren't even hurt. She's not the first and won't be the last to tell me to go fuck myself because I speak the truth. Don't stop it from being the truth. She gullible as hell. There's some lucky piece of shit out there just waiting to wife her."

"I'm not gullible. I just know people make mistakes is all."

"Okay, that's enough! We not here for this!" I shout, trying to stop the back and forth. I knew they would have a difference of opinion, which is why I didn't want to talk about this shit in the first place.

"I still think you should think about giving him another chance," Kēssa says.

"No, you should get you some new dicks and be happy!" Dena replies.

"Dang, y'all, we just broke up yesterday! Give me a minute to figure some shit out! All I'm thinking about right now is getting this house together. Which you're supposed to be helping me do. We haven't done shit since y'all got here. Come on." I end the conversation with that.

Dena tried getting up and stumbled back onto the couch. Now every time either of us tries getting to our feet, we all end up sitting back down, laughing uncontrollably. It takes us a good twenty minutes to finally get up and go to the main house to work. I hate getting the giggles.

Once we cure our munchies, I turn on that new Isley Brothers, *Body Kiss*. I play "Showdown Vol. 1" on repeat a few times. Though nobody was driving my car or wearing my clothes, I was still feeling Mr. Biggs on that song. We drank the rest of the wine and the next thing we knew, everything was in its place.

Before the ladies left, they asked me to promise to go out with them to Club Clymax next weekend. It's a new club I've been hearing a lot of good things about. Plays no rap music just R&B, which is cool with me. But I don't make promises I'm not sure I'm going to keep. Everything's so up in the air right now. They agreed to go together whether I go or not. They even exchanged numbers. Nice to see that my two friends like each other. We're finally all getting along. Maybe Kēssa will finally get Dena's name right.

I have so much to figure out. I'm not worried about the boys since I'm sure things will be pretty much like last time. Just more permanent. My main worry is what LaMar is going to do. Will he try to talk me into being with him again or will he let it go? Will I allow myself to give it another try? Is he as tired of me as I am of him? All I care about is peace. Peace of mind, peace in my home. Though I decided to end things, I wish he was here. We had good times through all those bad moments. And of course, I still love him.

Chapter 19

Let It Be

The next night, Momma calls me to let me know not to worry about the boys coming home. She's going to take them to school. I get a call from LaMar right after that. I almost don't answer the phone.

"Took you long enough. Thought I was going to voicemail." He still sounds like he's mad at me.

"I was working on some things around the house." I don't know why I feel I have to lie.

"Whatever. Do I get to pick up my sons tomorrow or is that a problem?"

"It's not a problem. I would like to pick them up though since they haven't seen their new rooms yet." Long silence. "Hello?"

"I heard you." More silence. "You didn't have to do what you did." Here we go. The real reason he called. "If you didn't want to be with me anymore, all you had to do was say so."

"It wasn't that I didn't want you anymore. I was tired of waiting for you to understand that it's more to being a man and father than being there. You're the one who said you were tired of trying to live up to my idea of a man. I didn't want you to feel like I was trying to make you something that you're not. Plus, you know you busted yourself, right?"

"How's that?"

"Other females?"

"I told you that wasn't about nothing! That's not what I meant! How you gone hold that against me?"

"LaMar, we both know that was a Freudian slip. I'm not even mad. You're free to do whatever and whomever you'd like at this point."

"I don't even know what Freudian means. You're the one who has to trip every time something doesn't go your way!"

"Do you even realize how many times every time was? Do you have any idea how hard it is to be with someone who makes you feel like you're not worthy of having someone that has your back the same as you have theirs?"

"I had your back in every way but financially! You make plenty of money! Me not working wasn't hurting you none! I know one thing, I'll never be with another boujee-ass female again!"

"Call me whatever you like, but this was never about money! This was about responsibility! And the fact that you don't see that further proves I made the right decision!"

"So that's it? We're not going to see what happens? You done? It's over?"

This argument, like so many others, isn't going anywhere. He never feels understood and neither do I. All this yelling needs to stop.

I give myself a minute before answering him and calmly say, "Yeah, I'm good. We cool. I'm not holding no grudges and I would hope, when you can get to that place, you won't either."

"I got a reason to be mad, T! You up and disappeared! The way you left was so disrespectful! That hurt me! To come home and see your family gone without you! That was fucked up! I wouldn't have done you like that, and you know it! And you promised you'd never do that to me! You lied!"

"I'll admit that shit was petty. But you gotta understand I was hurt too."

"But I'm asking, what do we do now? Do we wait awhile and try again or not?"

"I don't think we're good for each other. I'm not saying either of us was right or wrong. You have your faults and I have mine. I don't want to fight anymore, LaMar. I'm tired."

"And so you can say 'fuck him,' just like that?"

"It wasn't a 'just like that' thing. This has been building. The fact you couldn't keep a job . . . problem. You let me go through the whole house thing alone . . . problem. Me not trusting you . . . problem."

"So, we can't work through those things?"

"I tried to talk to you about how I'm feeling, and it seemed to go in one ear and out the other. How long am I supposed to try with you and you're not trying with me? I don't know what the future holds, but all I want now is for us to co-parent and respect each other. Maybe we can be friends."

"I see that you're not ready to talk about this right now. I'll get with you on this when you stop trippin'! Let me know when I can get the boys!"

Click.

He didn't listen this time either. At least I don't feel like crying.

I SLEPT WELL LAST NIGHT DESPITE MY CONVERSATION with LaMar. My mattress is magical. I step outside to leave for work and the sun is shining. When I start my car, I see that I have a full tank of gas. Life is good. I turn on the radio, and it's already tuned to AM1140.

"Good morning, OKC! It's going to be a beautiful day, so don't let work keep you inside! Someone called in and requested this song. It's an old one but good one . . . I guess she needs to know why. Here's Keith Sweat to help ask that question."

And Keith Sweat's "Why Me, Baby" comes on.

Now, why he do that? Tears fill my eyes and I hurry and turn the radio off. I manage to hold back tears but when I park at work and look in the mirror my eyes are on fire! I snap the mirror closed and dig around in my purse looking for Visine—you know to get the red out—and the tears start to flow but this time I can't stop them. A few people see me and wave as they are going in, but I guess they can't see what state I'm in. I wave back and manage a fake smile. I give myself time, take a few breaths, and talk to myself.

"Toi, you got this. It's a beautiful day, and you're not going to sit here feeling sorry for yourself." And when that doesn't work, "Bitch, get yo' ass out this car and stop thinking about that man! He's a cheating, no-working asshole, remember?"

That does it. I suck up my tears and go inside. I'm functioning, but I don't feel like myself. Somehow, Dena must have sensed it, because she comes busting up in my office as she likes to do without knocking.

"What's wrong with you? Why are you sitting there with resting bitch face? You too cute for that."

"Dena, I'm working, that's all. Am I supposed to be sitting here smiling like a Cheshire cat?" As my mother would say.

"Hell, yeah! You have a beautiful new home, cute and smart boys, a good job, newfound freedom, and the most amazing best friend anyone could ever have! Someone with all that should never not have a smile on their face!"

"I'm just tired."

"Lies!" She says it so loud it made me jump. "You got that wonderful new bed! You're not tired! You got I'm-newly-single-itus! Your ass is missing LaMar! Please say it ain't so!" She looks at me with disappointment written on her face.

"I will say whatever you want if you'd please lower your damn voice!" I grunt at her.

She ducks her head and brings her voice down to almost a whisper. "Oh, my bad. Was I yelling?"

"Pretty much. But yes, I do miss him. I'm not wanting him

back, but hearing his voice last night did make me want to see him. He was so hurt, Dena."

"What the hell he want already? Can't he give you a minute? Dang!"

"He wanted to know if he could get the boys and why I did him like that."

"Like what?"

"Why I left him the way I did."

"I hope you told him it was because he doesn't deserve you and you were tired of his shit!"

"Not quite what I said, but something like that. He did make me feel bad though for doing what I did."

"Why? You tried talking to him. He thought you were still drinking that spring water and he had you sprung. Just don't fall for the bull."

"I'm not, but it will take some time for me to truly move on. It's not like I didn't love him. Still do. We were growing differently."

"Growing differently, hell! You were growing and he was going backwards. Like you said, you had three kids instead of two. The only thing is you were molesting that oldest one."

"Dena, don't be saying shit like that."

"I'm just saying. That's why you need to get out and see what's out there. What did your momma say when I left Keyon? The best way to get over one man is to get under another one. It works too. Worked very well for me. And after I got under that one, I realized I can get under as many as I wanted. It's a wonderful thing! That's why I came in here, to see if you're going out with Kēssa and me this coming weekend."

"I doubt it. We'll see."

She turns up her lip in disgust. "You get on my nerves. Bye." And she storms out as she stormed in.

~

MOMMA PICKED THE BOYS UP FOR ME SINCE I GOT OFF A little late. That gave me time to get home and give the boys' rooms a once-over before she brought them home. I'm so excited for them to see their new rooms.

The alarm says, *front door open*. I greet them coming in the door.

"Mommy!" they both scream. Momma comes in the door behind them. This is her first time back to the house since she helped me move.

"Baby, this is beautiful!" She smiles, scanning the room.

LJ jumps with excitement. "Mommy, this is the house I wanted!"

"Me too!" Ty says, joining him.

"I know. I had to get it because my babies wanted it. Let's go look at your rooms!"

I take them both by their hands and lead them down the hall. We get to Ty's room first.

"Ohhhh, my room is blue!" he says in awe. He goes in and looks into the closet and his toy box. "All my stuff is in here, LJ, not yours. This my room." He tries to push his brother out of the room.

"Stop, Ty!" LJ pushes back.

"He knows it's your room, stop that!" Momma says, chastising Ty and grabbing his hand.

"I want to see my room, Mommy!" LJ runs to the next room. "Is this one mine?" he asks, eyes wide.

"Yelp."

He opens the door, and his mouth flies open. "This is A-MAZING! It's the best room I've ever seen!" He and Ty both run in and start touching stuff. "Thank you, Mommy! I love it!" He comes over and hugs me. I knew he would. They have a nice-sized area for their toys and plenty to do in each room. Seeing their faces glow made me so proud of myself. With the boys playing in LJ's room, I show Momma the rest of the house.

After the tour, we go into the kitchen for tea. "I'm kinda jealous. Your house is way nicer than mine. I'm so proud of you, baby."

"Thank you, Momma. The boys are happy, so I'm glad. I feel good right now."

"You should feel good. You're a great mom."

"I hate they couldn't have their dad here with them. I don't know how long it'll be before they start wondering where he is."

"Don't stress yourself about it. It's going to be what it is. I hate it too, but what you going to do, stay unhappy for the kids? That's not going to help anyone." She takes a gulp of her tea and lets out a loud "ahhh" then looks at the glass before putting it down. Why do we look at our drink after it hits the spot? "You know Dena called me and told on you."

"Oh my God, what I do?"

"She said you won't get under another man."

We both start laughing.

"Momma, it's too soon for all that."

"You take your time. You don't need a man. I told her crazy ass that so she would stop whining about being lonely. You know she don't have no damn sense."

Chapter 20

Last Chance

LaMar

The last few months have been hard as hell! Every time I saw Toi, I felt that knife she put in my back. It was like she didn't know she did anything wrong. All the arguing. We couldn't have a conversation without issues.

Things changed when she popped up at my graduation. She brought the boys and balloons. She showed so much support and let me know how proud she was of me. That's the Toi I know and love.

She took me out to celebrate, and we were able to sit down, laugh, talk, and spend that time together like a family. It just melted all my ice away. I was able to look at her and remember all the good times we had together. And I'm not gone lie, my dick got hard as hell. Her sitting across from me smiling again. I knew I saw that look in her eyes. She missed me. She tried to say it was because of the boys that she came. She wanted them to see their dad succeed—but I knew it was more to it.

I called her one night out the blue, and we talked for hours like we used to. Man, I was so busy being mad that I forgot how amazing she is.

Now we're hanging out. She let me know where she lives. It feels like we're dating again. It's just a matter of time before she lets me move into the house. And speaking of the house, it's the bomb! Hell, it feels like I elevate to a new level whenever I step in there. I can't wait to move in and invite my family over so they can see how we livin'. They gone be callin' *me* boujee next. I don't even mind the neighborhood at this point.

But as of right now we're just taking it slow. She not ready to say we're back together. Which is cool. I'm still doing me.

As a matter of fact, I'm on my way to meet her now. We're going to celebrate my new job as a computer programmer.

I go inside the restaurant, and she's already seated in a booth. When she spots me, she stands, waves, and throws that smile at me. Her jeans showing off her curves, red blouse unbuttoned just enough to let me get a peek of the red lacey bra she has on. Those caramel mounds jiggling a little as she waves. I feel my dick twitch in my jeans and have to adjust myself as I walk over to join her. When we hug, I feel the warmth of her breasts against my chest, and she smells like a damn vanilla cookie. I could skip dinner and go right to eating her.

"Have you been waiting long?" I ask as we sit down opposite each other.

"No, you're on time." Again, that smile. "I'm so excited for you, I'm not sure I can even eat anything."

"Whatever. You know you can't wait to get some steak."

"You picked Outback, not me."

"Yeah, well I couldn't wait to get steak either."

We order and talk about how my interview went and how I felt when I was told I got the position. After eating, we sit back and chill a minute.

"You look amazing, Toi. I don't think I've told you that tonight."

"Aww, thank you, LaMar." She looks at the waitress as she put the check on the table. She reaches over to pick it up.

"I got it," I said, pretending I can pay it.

"No, we're here to celebrate you."

"Naw, you pay and I won't hear the end of it." She lets me have the check. I look at it and slide it over to her. "Well, we are here to celebrate me."

"Yeah, that's what I thought."

She pays the check and hands it over to the waitress who hurries off.

"So, what are we going to do next? Go back to your house and have dessert?" I ask, watching her breasts rise and fall as she breathes.

"I'm not ready for all that, LaMar."

"Why not? We've been doing good. And I miss feeling you."

"I miss it too, but I don't know."

"Why you being like that?"

"I told you I don't want to rush into anything. Besides, I don't know what you got going on."

"Going on with what?"

"Other females."

"Man, I don't have nothing going on. I've been too busy finishing school and getting a job. And you say that like you haven't had the freedom to have been with someone else." I hold my breath waiting for her to answer. I'm praying she hasn't. No matter what we go through, that's mine. I can't stand the thought of anyone else getting that good stuff.

"I haven't. That's the last thing on my mind."

I let go of my breath and smile. "Well, okay then. So, until we figure out what it is we're going to do, let's agree that neither of us get with anyone else." I stick out my hand, and we shake on it.

I walk her out to her car. Before she gets in, I wrap my arms around her waist. She smiles as I hold her close to me. I look into her beautiful hazel eyes and see kindness and I feel like a piece of shit for everything I've put her through.

"Toi, I owe you an apology."

"For what?"

"For being a burden, for being immature, and for hurting

you. I never meant to do that. I know I don't deserve another chance, but things will be different if you can find it in your heart to forgive me. I've never had love like yours and contrary to what my actions have shown you in the past, I do love you. I will always love you. You have honestly been the best thing that has ever happened to me, and I'm a better man because of it."

Tears fill her eyes. She doesn't say anything but meets me halfway for a kiss.

She still didn't let me come over, but I know my girl. She wants it.

Toi

As time passed, I tried hard to be okay, but every time I saw LaMar I started to hurt all over again. Why couldn't he just do right? We could have had a great life together.

He was mad at me for months. He barely spoke to me and the way he looked when we'd meet up made me feel like I was the piece of shit. When we did talk, it always ended in an argument about who was wrong for what.

Recently things have switched. His smile is back. He apologized, and the boys love seeing us getting along.

We've been secretly going out and spending time together. There's no way I can let Dena or Momma know. Momma would probably get a switch, and Dena would probably slash my tires.

It's nice being with him, and there's something about being sneaky that makes it more exciting. But this time I'm taking things hella slow. When we went to celebrate him getting a job as a programmer, he tried it. But I wasn't ready. We did agree not to mess with anyone else until we figure out what we're doing.

So far things have been awesome. He's been attentive, charming, sweet, and loving. All the things that made my Tina Turner syndrome kick in in the first place. And since he's been so patient, I've decided it's been long enough. I told him to come over for dinner tonight. But I plan to be his dessert.

Kēssa has the boys. She's the only one that I could tell. And she's overly excited.

"That is so romantic. I knew y'all wouldn't just let it end like that. You two belong together. I don't know why you feel you should hide it. You're the one that has to deal with it."

"I still don't know if I want to get back with him. We're just seeing where it goes. If it works out, then I'll have to tell Momma. But if it doesn't, I never want this to come up. I'm trusting you."

"Girl, you don't have to worry about me saying nothing to no one. I'll play crazy when y'all announce to everyone y'all back together. And if that doesn't happen, well, neither did any of this."

"Thank you, sis."

~

THE PLAN IS TO SURPRISE HIM. I GOT EVERYTHING ready. I got something sexy to wear, a good slow-jam playlist, candles . . . shit, I forgot the wine!

It'll be a couple more hours before he gets here, so I need to run and get that.

I'm not going to lie—even though I'm nervous, I'm looking forward to being with him again. I can't help the huge smile on my face. It's not like the sex wasn't good. And it's been so long since I had some, it's crazy. Hell, a woman has needs. Who better than my babies' daddy to fulfill those needs?

I pull up to the liquor store and hurry inside. The weekends keep this placed packed. As I'm looking for my Twisted Sister, I hear a familiar laugh. I look up and see LaMar across the room. He must be here to get something for tonight too. I watch him and smile at how handsome he looks, standing there with a fresh cut. He's so damn sexy it's not even funny.

I almost call out his name, but I don't want to be all loud up in this store. I continue looking for what I need, thinking I'll just catch him at the register. When I look back up, some female I've never seen before walks over to him. He puts his arm around her and squeezes her ass, and she giggles. *The fuck?* I watch in shock while they talk, giggle, and walk up to the front together.

As they stand in line, he bends down and gives her a smack on the lips. Good thing I hadn't picked up anything or I would've dropped it—or thrown it at his ass. My heart sinks. I can't believe he's with another female just a couple of hours before he's supposed to be coming to be with me. I know we aren't together, but we had that discussion that we weren't going to see anyone else until we figure us out. I guess that was him saying *I* shouldn't be with nobody else. Clearly, he didn't mean him.

I watch as they make their purchase and go outside. I hurry over and stand in the window to see if they get into a car together. They do. Must be hers, which explains why I didn't see his car when I pulled up. Luckily for me, she parked right in front of the store. Before backing out, she leans over and kisses him passionately. The sight makes me sick to my stomach. I want to go out there and confront him. Instead I take pictures of them. I'm going to let him come on over and see how he's going to talk his way out of this shit.

As soon as they're gone, I hurry out the store and back home, mad at myself for even considering giving him another chance. Momma always said a leopard can't change their spots. I can't even think straight, I'm so angry. Why lie? I should have the choice to see others too if that's what we're doing. He's the one who suggested we don't. I guess what's good for the goose isn't good for the gander.

I get home and plop down on the couch, trying to breathe. How could he do that? What the hell is wrong with him? I'm so relieved that God showed me this before I let him touch me.

My hurt turns into anger, and I try to figure out how I'm going to show him the pictures I took of them. Do I do it as soon as he walks in? Do I ask questions first to see if he's going to lie?

As soon as it gets dark, he texts to let me know he's on his way.

I go in my room and put my sexy lingerie on. I make sure I smell good and look even better. I light the candles.

When I hear his car pull up, I turn the music on and dim the lights. He rings the doorbell. I open the door slowly. He didn't even bother to change clothes. He probably smells like her.

"Damn, baby! It's like that?" he asks, licking his lips and smiling.

I'm starting to hate that smile. "I thought I'd surprise you. You like?" I let him in and give him a spin.

"I love!" he says, smacking me on the ass. "Come give me a kiss." He grabs me and pulls me close.

I almost throw up.

"No." I turn my head to avoid his lips touching mine. "Not yet."

"Oh, so you gone tease a brother first, huh. I see how it is. You got it hooked up in here."

I take him by the hand and lead him over to the couch and push him down.

"You don't want to have a drink or something first?" he asks.

"Nope, I want to get right to the good part. It's been so long since I had you." I skip to his favorite song "Walked Out of Heaven" by Jagged Edge.

"You know that's my jam," he says, undressing me with his eyes.

"I know. That's why I picked it to dance for you." I begin to dance seductively.

He watches me with intent. I make sure to turn around a few times and bend over so he can get a full view of my ass that I'm about to tell him to kiss. Midway through the song, I walk over to him, climb into his lap, bounce up and down slowly. I put my breasts in his face.

"You smell so good." He closes his eyes, pressing his face into my breasts, inhaling me.

I continue my little tease. He grabs my ass and starts grinding against me. I can feel the hardness in his shorts.

"I want you so bad, Toi. I missed you so much," he whispers, kissing my neck.

He reaches up and grabs my breasts, squeezing them and rubbing my nipples through my lacy lingerie. Usually that would drive me insane and make me wet as hell. Right now, it's like the connection from my nipples to my clit has been severed. My pussy is never dry, but the more he touches me, the drier I'm getting.

He continues grinding. "You feel how hard you got me? Come on, baby. Stop teasing me. You know you want it. Let me slide this on up in you."

I'm cringing at his words, but I gotta play it cool.

"I want to show you something first." I climb off him, walk over to the table, and pick up my phone. I bring up the picture I took of him earlier, hide my phone behind my back, and walk back over to stand in front of him, smiling.

"What you got there? Another surprise?" he asks and grabs himself. He pets it as if he's telling it to heel. But I can see it's not obeying.

I pull out my phone and put the picture directly in his face. His mouth falls open. I pick up the remote and turn the music off. He sits back and shakes his head.

"Who is this, LaMar?" He keeps looking down and doesn't speak. "Imagine my surprise when I go to the liquor store preparing for tonight and see this. You don't have nothing to say?"

"I'm sorry." He shrugs.

"Yeah, you are. Deep inside I knew this wasn't going to work. I'm not going to let you hurt me ever again."

"Ain't nobody trying to hurt you. That's my friend."

"Once again, no accountability. Why did you even suggest we not see other people if you were just going to do it anyway?"

"Okay, my bad. It's not like me and you are back together. Technically, I didn't cheat. So why you mad?"

"Why am I mad? Really? You know what? I'm not mad, but I want you to leave."

"That don't even make no sense. It's not like I fucked her today. How you gone leave me all hard like this?" He grabs his erection again.

"Well, now you *can* go fuck her today. I got the dick ready for her. Bye, LaMar."

"Toi, wait—"

"No. Get out!" I point toward the door.

He sits here a couple more minutes before he can even look at me. I can see him thinking, but there's nothing he can say. Finally, he gets up and leaves.

HE CALLS ME DAYS LATER TRYING TO EXPLAIN HIMSELF, but I just hang up on him. There is nothing more for us to talk about other than our boys. He will never get this chance again. But what do I do now?

Chapter 21

Sad

I don't even care to hide my depression anymore. I have to work extra hard to let it not show around my kids, but they know something isn't right.

I was in the bed crying into my pillow the other night when LJ came into my room.

"Mommy, what's the matter?" he asked, climbing into my bed and wrapping his little arms around my neck.

"I'm okay, baby. Why are you up?" I said, trying to suck it up.

"I'm not sleepy cause I miss Daddy too." That made it worse. I turned over and held him. "Was Daddy bad? Is that why he don't live with us again?"

I didn't know how to answer that. I wanted to say yes, but would that cause him to feel a way about his dad? I didn't want him looking at LaMar differently.

"No, baby. Sometimes mommies and daddies aren't happy living together anymore. But me and your daddy still love you and Ty very much. And it has nothing to do with you or your brother. You guys are the greatest sons anyone could ever have."

"So y'all don't love each other no more?"

"I still love your daddy. That's why I'm sad that he's not here."

"Will he ever live here with us?"

"I don't think so, baby. But you'll still get to go see him all the time."

"Okay. But I hope you can stop being sad."

"Me too, baby. Me too." I kissed his little cheek before we both fell asleep.

~

IT'S BEEN HARD TO CONCENTRATE AT WORK AS WELL. I work from home a lot these days. Only go in if I absolutely have to. And when I do it's hard to be that ray of sunshine. I still make my rounds, but I usually do it with sunglasses on and a fake-ass smile. Then I hurry into my office, close the door, and stay in there, only leaving to go to the bathroom or home.

Ricky has noticed the change.

"Hey, Toi, you got a minute?" he asks, peeking his head in.

"Sure." I want to put my sunglasses back on. I'm sure my eyes look tired.

He sits across from me and stares but doesn't speak.

I put on my fake smile. "What's on your mind?"

"That."

"What?"

"That. That fake-ass smile."

"What?"

"You've been doing that for months now. Y'all have broken up before so why is this time so different? Last time you, me, and Dena would go out, kick it, have a good time. Now you don't want to do anything. We barely see you here. I ask you to go to lunch, you say you're busy. You haven't been answering our calls. What's up?"

"I guess I feel it more this time because I'm positive we won't get back together. I've been with him for eight years. That's not something that's easy to move on from overnight."

"I get that, but how are you supposed to move on if you

isolate yo'self and wallow in it? Y'all haven't been together for a minute now. You gotta do something to move forward. Sitting around with yo' shoulda, coulda, wouldas isn't going to help."

"I hear you."

"Good. Then let me put a smile on your face. Come to lunch with me."

"I don't know. I really do have a lot of work to do."

"Damn shame. But I won't pressure you." He gets up and leaves.

About twenty minutes later, here comes Dena and she doesn't bother to knock.

I force my smile back in place. "Hey, siss—"

"Don't 'Hey, sissy' me!" She closes the door.

"What I do?"

"I'm sick of this sad-ass Toi. I want my friend back!"

"What are you talking about?"

"You walk around here looking like a sad little puppy throwing that fake smile at everybody. Everybody's talking about it. You not foolin' no one. You won't hang out. When we do talk, it's either about that thang you once called your man, or you don't have nothing to say. Ricky told me he came in here and you blew him off." She pointed at the side window. "You don't even have yo' blinds open so you can see Craven." She walks over and opens them.

He looks up as if he sensed it and waves. We both wave back.

Dena smiles. "Now doesn't that feel better? Just look at him. Sitting over there, bald head shining. I can see his dimples from here. You're depriving yourself of all joys in life." She walks over to me, takes me by the shoulders, and shakes me. "Snap out of it!" She slaps me. Not hard but I felt it. "Y'all broke up! He didn't die! You don't need to be grieving him like this! He cheated on you, he wouldn't take care of you, he messed this up! Wake the fuck up, please!"

"I know, okay? But knowing doesn't change the fact that I loved him," I say, catching my tear before it fell. "I loved the hell out that man! I birthed two amazing little boys for him. I was faithful and loyal. All I asked for in return was for him to love me back and he didn't, D. He didn't love me back! Why didn't he love me?" I start crying. Hard.

Dena rushes over to the window and closes the blinds and rushes back to hug me. "He did love you, sis. He just didn't know how to do it right."

I cry for I don't know how long.

"Sissy. Please come over to my house tonight. I already called Momma J, and she's going to get the boys," she says, rocking me.

"Okay."

"Okay?"

"Yes. Okay."

Chapter 22

Made Up Day

I get over to Dena's and notice that Kēssa's car is here as well. I get a funny feeling and almost pull off, but I know I would never hear the end of it. So, I park and get out.

"SURPRISE!" they yell when I walk in.

"It's not my birthday. What is this?"

"It's your Brand-New Day day," Dena answers and blows a party favor.

"My what?"

They begin to dance around the room, flailing their arms around, singing, *Can you . . . feel a . . . brand new daaay.* Over and over. They look so silly with their pointy party hats, singing all loud. I had no choice but to laugh.

"That's the first genuine smile I've seen from you in months," Dena says.

"Thanks, guys. But I still don't get it."

"Today we want to help you move forward. We need to get you to see your blessings so you can let go of that hot mess of a relationship you had."

"Yeah, sis, even I know you deserve better," Kēssa adds, which shocks me since she has always been team LaMar.

They each come and give me a hug.

"I love you," Kēssa says.

"You're amazing," Dena says. "Okay, now come take your seat."

Dena pushes me over to a chair in the middle of the room and places a crown on my head. I look around. They have balloons, food, and drinks. And on the wall is a Pin the Tail on the Donkey game—but it has LaMar's face instead of a donkey.

"Where did you get that picture of LaMar?" I ask Dena.

"From yo' house. Along with the three T-shirts that I know isn't yours." She holds them up.

"Wait, what are we doing with those? I sleep in those. They're comfortable."

"They also belong to him. It's bad juju to keep them. That's why we're going to burn them in the fire pit later. Need to rid you of all his energy. But first, a toast!" Dena hands me a shot glass bigger than theirs. It smells strong.

"What is this?" I ask, sniffing at it again.

"Tequila." She hands me a lime and salt.

"This is a lot of tequila. You know I'm a lightweight."

"You'll be fine. Now, let's toast to recovery!"

They take their shots to the head, and I try to sip at mine but Dena tips it into my mouth. I gag some and swallow it down quickly, licking the salt and sucking on the lime.

"Alright, let's party!"

We smoke a blunt after the shot, and I'm feeling pretty good. We play Pin the Tail on the Donkey and end up pinning it to his face mostly. We eat, then smoke again and sing songs that were all pretty much "fuck you" songs such as "Tyrone" by Erykah Badu. And when we sing it, we sing it loud and proud. I must admit I feel like it's starting to work. But I'm so tipsy, who knows.

We're about to go do the burning of the T-shirts when Ricky walks in.

"I didn't think you were going to make it," Dena says.

"I didn't want to miss Toi's Brand-New Day day." He laughed.

"Hi! I'm Kēssa." She steps over to Ricky, hand extended.

"Nice to meet you." He shakes her hand and tries to let go but she has a grip on it, just looking at him, smiling all weird. That's her "I want you" look. The man has to practically pry her hand off his.

He comes over, hugs me tight and close, and whispers, "If you need to get under me to get over him, I'm here for it."

"I see Dena has been in your ear."

He joins us outside for the burning of the T-shirts.

Before I place them into the fire I say, "I release myself from the hold you have on me. I deserve to be loved properly. I appreciate parts of what we had, but I now give myself permission to move on to better things." Then I place each one into the fire. We sit outside and watch them burn. It feels good, I admit.

We go back inside, have more drinks, and smoke. Ricky leaves first.

"So, what's up with him? He's fine as hell!" Kēssa says after he walks out the door.

"Girl, you're not ready for that kind of man," Dena tells her.

"Why you say that? He looks like something I can handle."

"Because he's not the type to be with someone who *needs* a man. You don't want to get attached to him. He'd definitely break your heart and yo' face."

Kēssa rolls her eyes. "You always got something to say."

"That's because what I say needs to be said."

I END UP STAYING AT DENA'S. BEFORE PASSING OUT, I think about how blessed I am. I have so much love from my friends and family. I have my wonderful sons. And LaMar wasn't for me. I should be happy that ended. What have I been crying over?

Chapter 23

I'm Done

It's been a few weeks since the Brand-New Day day, and I'm not going to lie—that little ritual seems to have helped. I feel a lot better. I got my energy back. I haven't cried not one time since then. Actually, the feelings went from sad to kinda mad at myself for crying over that boy for so long. I still have my days where I miss him, but when I do I slap myself out of it like Dena showed me.

I got my Sunshine title back at work. I still don't fully feel back to normal, but I know that'll come in time. What matters right now is that my kids are happy, I'm getting out of the house again, and I'm no longer moping around. But what really solidified it for me is the other day when LaMar came over to pick up the boys.

He came in and the boys greeted him at the door as usual.

"I see y'all ready to go." He smiled down on them.

"Yes, sir," LJ said, smiling with his bag in hand.

"Okay, y'all go play in y'alls' rooms. I need to talk to yo' momma for a minute."

They left their bags by the door and ran to the back.

"What you need to talk to me about?"

"Can we go back there to your bedroom, out of ear range of the kids, please?"

I didn't think nothing of it and had him follow me back.

"Now what—" Before I could fully turn around, he grabbed me and kissed me. I immediately pushed him off. "Boy, what are you doing?"

"I still love you, T. You won't listen to anything I have to say. I'm a changed man I swear!" he said, crossing his heart. "I think if we make love, you'll see you still love me too and we can move forward."

"We are moving forward, just not together. Did you really think you were going to bring me back here, kiss me, and I was just going to rip my clothes off for you?"

"That was pretty much the plan, yeah. Baby . . ." He grabbed me, and again I pushed him away. He grabbed me again and locked his arms around my waist. "Look me in the eyes and tell me you don't love me anymore."

I looked him dead in his eyes. "I don't love you anymore."

He let me go, stepped back, cocked his head to the side with his mouth hanging open. "You said that like you mean it."

"I mean it, LaMar. I don't. I don't love you, I don't want you, and I don't need you."

"Damn, T. It's like that? I know I hurt you but—"

"But nothing. All you need to understand is that you hurt me. Not once but multiple times. I told you I would not give you a chance to do it again and I meant that. So, let's get an understanding right now. We're going to be cordial, we're going to co-parent, and we're going to live our best lives separately. I don't hate you and hope that someday we can be friends. But there is and will never be a you and me ever again. And I put that on everything I love."

"You shouldn't say never, but I hear you. I'm not going to give up just like that. I'm gone always love you."

"I love you too—as the father of my children. But as far as a relationship, that's done. I'm done."

"So why can't we do it one more time? You know, for closure. You scared all the feelings will come flooding back, and you'll have to take that 'never' back?"

"This conversation has given me all the closure I needed. I'm not going to have sex with you. Not because I'm scared of my feelings returning but because you just don't do it for me anymore."

"Damn, that was harsh. I guess I better go then."

"Have fun with the boys." I smiled and waved. I let him see himself out.

When I tell y'all that when he left with his tail between his legs I felt better than I ever had before, I'm not even lying. Tellin' him to his face that I didn't desire him made me realize I truly didn't. My nipples didn't even get hard when he kissed me. I was so proud of myself.

Guess who I called after he left.

"So, he tried to use his penis to dickmatize you again?" Dena said when I told her what had happened.

"Girl, this man was confident that all it would take is for me to lay down with him and just like that we're back together like nothing even happened. Tried to bait me in with the 'oh you scared' bull crap."

"Hey, you can't blame the dog for trying. Enough about him. I met me a new dude."

"Oh shoot. He's not a 'hit it and quit it' one?"

"No, I actually like this one. His name is Tao. He's African and has the sexiest accent. It's heavy and I have to have him repeat himself most times, but I don't mind since I like the way he sounds."

"Awww, I'm excited for you."

"I know, right? Me too."

I'm glad one of us has been able to move on to the point where they can see themselves with someone else. I'm definitely not there yet. But I'm proud of where I am. I'm going to be able to move on and figure out what I truly want. But for now, I'm going to chill and enjoy me. No need to bring a man into this.

Chapter 24

What Do We Have Here

Things haven't been too hard with the day-to-day stuff, but my feelings are still hurt. I have to work hard every time I see LaMar not to be mean. He's still trying to get me to change my mind, but that's not happening. We have a good routine now and the boys are in a good place with the way things are. Momma and Dena have been a great deal of help, giving me breaks if I need it, coming over and keeping me company. Even Kēssa has been coming around more. Happy to have my village.

My personal life has been quite boring. I'm not dating at all. I'm not in the mood. I'm still angry by the way things went down and have developed trust issues. I took a work trip to New Orleans a little bit ago. That had me thinking I was getting over it, but I'm not. Not going to say much more about that trip. I don't want to think about it. Not even Dena knows what happened.

Work is work of course. I've been keeping myself busy, so I don't have to think too much. Craven's department has merged with ours, which has been interesting. I still don't know a lot about him. I've heard rumors of him being considered a Bible thumper. They say it's because he carries a Bible around all the time. People always got something to say.

For the past month, he's been sitting across from me in every meeting, every week. He's even finer up close. He's probably about 6'4" or taller, has pecan-colored skin and it's silky too. Bald head, goatee, and lips so juicy you want to suck on them. His eyes are light brown when the light hits them right, and he has these dark, long eyelashes that would make any woman jealous. His smile shows off these two deep dimples. Gets me wet every time he shines it at me. And he's always dressed nice and smells good. I find myself staring at him with Jill Scott's "All I" playing in my head. When he catches me staring, I quickly avert my attention elsewhere. I haven't seen this Bible yet. But he definitely has a ring on his finger, so all I can do is look.

This morning, I open my emails and I see one from him. Of course, I'm surprised because we aren't working directly with each other. Maybe he has a question.

Good morning, Toi,

I'm sure this is going to be strange to you, getting an email from me since we don't really know each other. I've noticed you haven't been the same ray of sunshine you used to be when coming through the office and I'm worried about what you might be going through. I don't want to get into your business or anything like that, but I would like to talk to you to see if there's anything I could do to help.

If nothing else, I could pray with you. Just let me know. Enjoy your day and please show your beautiful smile.

Craven

I am beyond flattered to say the least. I didn't think he thought of me one way or the other. The most he's ever said to me is a "good morning" or "have a nice day." And don't think I didn't notice he called my smile beautiful. I read that part twice. I know he's just being nice, but the way my imagination works . . .

I email him back and thank him for his concern. I let him know it would be nice to sit down and talk with him at lunch. He agrees to meet me in the break room.

I call Dena. She knows I've been craving Craven. Get it?

"Girl, guess who sent me a random email saying they want to sit down with me."

"LaMar?"

"Naw, why would he be emailing me?"

"Well, he can't get you to do what he wants any other way. So why not email."

"Ugh, you're ruining this for me." Silence. No other guesses. I blurt out, "Craven."

"Hold up! What? Cravin' Craven? You lying! What did he say?"

"I'll forward you the email." She doesn't say anything. "Did you get it?"

"Yeah, shhh. I'm reading." Silence. "Oh my God! What the hell? Is he trying to holla?"

"I doubt it. He's married, right?"

"Yeah, I think so. He has a ring on, but I know him as well as you. All I'm sure about is that he's fine as hell!"

"Well, I'm going to meet him for lunch."

"Bitch, you betta tell me what happens!"

"I can tell you now. We're going to talk. What else could happen?"

"Whatever it is, I want to know about it. If he licks his lips, I want to know about it. If he blinks in slow motion, I want to know about it. If he touches you , I want to know about it. As a matter of fact, I'll be at your house after work."

"Why don't you come down and sit across from us? That way you can see what happens with your own eyes."

"Don't test me, woman!" Dena warns.

"Okay, chill. I'm sure there will be nothing to tell, but I'll tell you when you get to my house, whatever nothing there is."

"That's what I wanted to hear." And she hangs up.

With lunchtime approaching, I start to get nervous. I have no idea what to expect. I keep reminding myself that he's only being nice. Still, I make sure my hair and makeup are on point and spray on a little of my vanilla body spray. Right before I lock my computer, he sends me another email:

Hey, making sure we're still meeting. Looking forward to getting to know you.

I let him know I'm on my way over there and hurry out the door.

When I walk in, I don't see him. I guess I'm more excited about meeting up than he is. I walk around the corner to the quiet rooms and spot him through one of the little windows. He sees me at the same time. Standing, he quickly opens the door for me before I can get to it. As I squeeze by him, I smell his cologne and whatever it is makes my mouth water just a little bit. He pulls out the chair across from him for me to sit in.

"Well, hello, lady. I see you're wearing that smile I asked for," he says through his smile.

Damn, this man is so freaking sexy!

"It was very nice of you to be so concerned about me since I'm a stranger. It's unexpected and appreciated."

"I don't think of you as a stranger. Just a friend I haven't spent time with yet." Can he hear my heart beating fast? I can. "We've been working in the same office for years. I don't know why we haven't done this before." He leans toward me. "I'm glad you're here now. So, what's been going on? Are you okay?"

"I'm okay. Going through some things in my personal life I'm not completely over yet. But I'm getting there. I honestly thought my demeanor had changed drastically. I'm surprised you saw anything."

"Well, I noticed when it first started months ago. No smile, barely coming in to work, blinds always closed. I used to look forward to seeing you throughout the day. But I have recently seen the change. You've even been opening your blinds again. But I can still see that you're troubled sometimes. Can I ask what's been going on?"

"I had to separate from the father of my two boys. We're doing well with co-parenting right now, though."

"So sorry to hear that. I know that can put a strain on you. I take it that's why your energy has been off. Do you mind if I pray with you?" he asks with concern in his eyes.

"Of course not."

He grabs both my hands, and we bow our heads.

"Almighty God, we come to you with our hearts open, asking that you grant this young woman peace of mind and an end to her sadness. Give her strength and clarity in all questions that may still linger in her mind and help her to understand that you make no mistakes. Fill her with your light, dear God, and give her strength when she is weak and comfort when she is alone. Bless her boys to grow up smart and strong despite the brokenness of the home. Help her to keep her faith in love. And God, for me, please give her a reason to smile again. In Jesus's name, we pray. Amen."

"Amen."

No one has ever done this for me before, and I tear up a little. I look up at him. He's still holding my hands and the warmth feels so good. The way he's staring into my eyes makes me feel safe.

"I pray that helps you feel a little better." Finally letting go of my hands, he reaches into his pocket and pulls out his card. "Here's my cell number. You can text me if you need to."

I can't believe he passed me his number. Why am I getting so excited over this married man?

"Your wife not going to have an issue if I text you?"

"No, you don't have to worry about that."

We continue talking about work, the merger, and our personal lives until the hour is up. When I get back to my office, my face is hurting, I'm smiling so much. He's easy to talk to. I didn't feel judged, which I expected from a so-called Bible thumper. The good feelings last me all day.

By the time I pick up the boys and get home, Dena is already sitting in the driveway waiting for me. She hops out of her car as soon as I pull up.

"Momma, Auntie D here," Ty announces, stating the obvious.

"Hey, my babies!" she says as they both run over to hug her. She leans back in her car and pulls out a bag. "I got y'all those Transformers you wanted. Here!"

They each grab a bag and look inside. "Thank you, Auntie D!" LJ shouts. "Momma, can I open this when I get in the house, pleeease?"

"Yeah, can we?" Ty asks.

Dena answers for me. "Come on, y'all, I'll help you open them."

They walk in without even looking back at me. It's Friday, so I allow it. I'm waiting for their dad to come to pick them up. We weren't in the house a good twenty minutes before LaMar rings the doorbell.

Dena beats me to the door and swings it open aggressively.

"Well, look who's here." She stands with one hand on her hip and a disgruntled look on her face. This is the first time they've seen each other since everything that happened had happened. I stay in the hall.

LaMar pushes past her. "Where's Toi?"

"She's back there getting the boys' stuff together." She's still looking at him with a stank face.

"Why you lookin' all ugly like that?" Now he's frowning up himself.

"I don't know what it is about you I don't like. Oh yeah, you're a hoe. That's it!" She snaps her fingers like that suddenly came to her.

"I'm not too fond of you myself. You always over here! You homeless?"

"No, I'm wanted here. I am always welcome!"

"Whatever, man! Why don't you gone somewhere and smoke? I'm sure it's been more than five minutes and you're probably going through withdrawals by now."

"You right. I wish I would've lit something up before you got here . . . like some sage."

I hurry the boys before it gets ugly. We come around the corner and of course, they are happy to see their dad. They always overreact when they greet people.

"Daddy!" they sing in unison and hug his legs, almost knocking him over. He's still in his feelings and both him and Dena are looking at each other crazy.

"Y'all need to cut that out," I say.

"Your friend always coming for me. She gets on my nerves." LaMar looks her up and down.

"I get on your nerves, huh? Well—"

"Dena, go to the Toibox and wait for me please."

"But let me just say how trif—"

"Nope. Toibox. Go, please."

I cut her off because I'm sure whatever she's about to say next isn't going to do anything but make things worse. She walks away, mumbling something under her breath and rolling her neck.

"I don't know why you let her bother you," I say to LaMar.

"I'm not thinking about her. What's up with this Toibox?"

"Oh, that's what I call my small guesthouse in the back. That's where we chill at."

"When do I get to chillax in the Toibox?" He steps closer to me, undressing me with his eyes.

"Never!" Dena yells from the kitchen.

"Toibox, D!!" I yell back at her.

"Okay! Dang!"

"Anyways, when are you bringing them back?" I inquire, changing the subject.

"Oh, so you just going to ignore my question? I see how it is. Probably keep them this whole week."

"Okay, y'all have fun."

"You know I miss you, right?" He steps closer, giving me that look that used to get me every time. But now I feel nothing. Not even a slight tingle.

"Bye, Lamar!" Dena shouts from the kitchen again. "I know, I know . . . Toibox, D," she says before I can.

"She always blockin'! Man, I'll see you later." He turns to the door and shrieks at the boys as they are chasing each other in the front yard. "Boys, y'all come say bye to your momma!"

I kiss and hug our babies goodbye and head out to the Toibox. Dena is sitting with her lighter at the ready and as soon as I walk in, she flick her Bic.

"Sooo . . . what he do?"

"Who, LaMar?"

"You know damn well I'm not talking about no damn LaMar. What happened with Craven?"

"Nothing really. We talked about a little bit of everything. He asked if he could pray with me. I said yes, of course, and we held hands and bowed our heads. It was a beautiful prayer. Almost made me cry. He did hold on to my hands a minute after." Under my breath, fast and low, I add, "He gave me his number to text him." I raise my voice back up. "He's a cool guy."

"Wait, wait. Did I hear you say he gave you his number? How he gone do that? He married, right?"

"Yeah, but he said not to worry about that. He has plenty of friends he communicates and prays with. He wants to be friends. Not like he wants to hook up with me."

Side-eyeing me, she says, "So, he hits you up out of the blue and asks you to have lunch with him, holds on to your hands a minute after the prayer—I know you thought I didn't hear that— then gives you his number, and he merely wants to be friends?"

"Don't start, Dena. That man don't want me."

"If you say so. Remember I said otherwise."

My phone pings. It's Craven.

HRY?

I'm good, sitting here tlkin to Cadena. HRY?

> I'm great. Just chking on u. Hope ur still wearing that smile. Tell Cadena I said hi. Hit me up when u get time.

"That's him, huh? I can tell by the way you over there grinning."

"Yeah, he's making sure I'm good. I don't know what it is about him, but I get butterflies getting his texts."

"I know what it is. He's fine as hell, and you've been sitting across from him for . . . what, a month or so, fantasying about doing all kinds of nas-ty stuff to him. You need Jesus."

"I know, right? Glad he doesn't know about that. I like the idea of us being friends. Maybe he'll do something to make me mentally put him in the friend zone. Because I'm tired of daydreaming about him."

Later that night I catch myself fantasying about him again, wishing I knew how it was to kiss and touch him. I mean a girl can dream, right? It does help me realize that I still have desires and that I would like to spend time with someone. Not in another relationship but just someone to kick it with and have fun. Maybe go out on a few dates or something. I'm still not rushing into anything, but maybe it is about time I get out there. See, what had happened was . . .

About the Author

Ah'shay Young believes in the power of friendship, even when happily ever after doesn't work out. When she's not writing books, she enjoys painting, going to poetry nights, spending time with her two grandsons, Adrian Jay and Caire, and meditating. *What Had Happened Was* is the debut novel in her new series. She lives in Oklahoma with her family.

More by Admission Press

Looking for your next great read?
Visit www.admissionpress.com